OUT OF TIME

MARK SAVAGE

DEDICATION

My mother would not have been surprised to hear that I've written a novel. Amused possibly, but not surprised. My ideas often amused her. I'm sure she suspected her middle child was a bit off his rocker. However, she would have been encouraging. She always was. This one's for you, Mom.

OUT OF TIME

ACKNOWLEDGMENTS

I am fortunate to have a group of friends that are not only a hell of a lot of fun to hang around with but are always a very supportive bunch as well. Thanks, gang! I hope you all know you're appreciated. I'm grateful also for those people on social media who have shown an interest in this new venture of mine.

A few people, in particular, I would like to thank. Anne Allen and Kyle Wilhelm, who, after reading the first draft of part one, encouraged me to keep working and finish the book. They were probably just being nice, but, if not for them, I might still be writing a chapter or two a month. Robert Weitzel, who read an early draft of the whole story and advised me to, "Just publish the damn thing!" And Barb Parr, who was kind enough to do a final proofing of the manuscript.

PART ONE

CHAPTER ONE

Looking back on it, dying was nothing like what I'd expected. Not that I'd spent a lot of time thinking about dying. Even at ninety-one years of age, I had never felt that death was lurking just around the corner. I was in better shape than most people fifteen years younger than me and, in fact, I felt kind of guilty when people around me complained about their health; like it was somehow my fault that they were in such bad shape and I wasn't. And there were people around me complaining. I'd been living in a senior's condominium where, for some, complaining was a popular pastime.

But, as I said, I was in pretty good shape for a guy my age, so it's not like I just wasted away. No, when I went out, it was with a bang, that being the sound the car made when it hit the embankment and was launched into the air. The sound it made when it hit the ground again was a bit more of a grinding, tearing noise. The sound I made when the car left the ground was kind of a little-girl-like scream. I don't know what noise I made when the car landed, but I'm guessing it wasn't pleasant.

When I regained consciousness, I was hanging from the seat belt. The world was utterly black, and there was a dripping sound somewhere close by. A ringing in my ears and a pulsating pain in my head made me feel like I was going to be sick. When it sunk into my throbbing head that the dripping sound was my own blood, I realized how bad my situation really was.

Oh God! I thought. *I'm dying!*

I was dying, and apart from wishing the God-awful sick feeling would go away, the only thing I could think about was what people were going to say. Stupid, I know, but I hated that people were likely going to ask why the hell a ninety-one-year-old guy was driving in the first place. Fact is, I am, was, a good driver! Shit! Am? Was? What verb do you use when you used to be an old man and then you died and now you're young and, damnit, you don't know what the hell is going on? And what's with all this darned swearing? In all my years I was never one to curse much, and now I can't seem to bloody stop! Maybe I'm not me after all, if that makes any sense.

So, it was a Sunday morning in June, and I was out for a drive because, well, what else do you do when you're my age, and almost every friend you've ever had has either kicked the bucket or lost his marbles? The activities at the condo bored the crap out of me and driving had always been one of my favourite pastimes, especially early morning drives. There's nothing like being out on the highway when the sun has just come up, the air is fresh, and the highway is practically void of cars. Granted, in recent years it's not often that any road is traffic free. When I first started enjoying a highway drive, back in my thirties, the road was always deserted in the morning. Oh, occasionally you'd encounter a farmer moving some equipment from one piece of land to another, but you'd wave and get a wave back and then you were past him and enjoying the open road again. Nowadays, no one waves anymore. In fact, you're lucky if the people you meet even look up from their damned cell phones long enough to remember that they are in control of a bloody vehicle. Sorry. One of my pet peeves. People whose entire life is spent with their eyes glued to those damned cell phones. It's not just a little ironic then that that's what got me in the end.

I was on Highway 5, East of Saskatoon, pretty early that morning. It was always a fun road to drive, because of its rolling hills. In recent years, it became one of the more dangerous roads because of those hills, and unlike most Saskatchewan highways, it had next to nothing for a shoulder.

It was right at the crest of one of those hills that it happened. A young woman with her SUV full of kids came over the hill and, sure as hell, she was looking at her damned cell phone as she drove right at me down the middle of the road. I didn't even have time to hit the horn. I swerved and caught the edge of the asphalt with my front tire, and as I tried to fight the car back onto the road, I lost control of it and shot towards the ditch.

I might have been fine if the ditch was clear, but as luck would have it, I hit it right where a small road met the highway. It was like hitting a ramp at the wrong angle doing over one hundred kilometres an hour. Actually, it was hitting a ramp at the wrong angle doing over one hundred kilometres an hour. It was the end of me, and I don't think the woman in the SUV ever knew that she killed me. I probably saved the lives of everyone in that vehicle but ended my own in the process.

In case you're wondering, my entire life didn't flash before my eyes in the last few seconds. Thank God! I would probably have died from boredom. Not that I'd had a bad life. It's just that there wasn't anything significant about it. Pathetic, really, that in ninety-one years of life, nothing had ever happened that was worth writing about.

There was a white light at the end though, or maybe what

was better described as a white flash. But there were no loved ones inside of it reaching out and calling to me. Just a flash of white at the very end and my life was over.

 And then I woke up.

I awakened lying in the ditch a few feet from the car. At first, I wondered if I'd been saved by someone, freed from the vehicle and revived, most likely to spend my remaining days in a wheelchair. I groaned inwardly at the thought. It would have been better if they'd let me die. But then I realized I was alone.

In retrospect, I did notice as I pushed myself up off the ground that my hands were not the hands of an old man. Not the wrinkled and knobby hands I'd grown used to, but the smooth, strong hands of a youth. But I was too confused at the time for that fact to sink in.

My body was stiff, probably from lying in a cold ditch for – how long? I had no way of knowing, but it was still early enough that the sun had not yet begun to warm the cool grass where I was lying. As I stood and stretched, I was totally flabbergasted that I was seemingly unhurt. How could I be unhurt? How could I have gotten out of the car? Why wasn't I standing in line waiting to make my excuses to an ancient and eternally bored Saint Peter? What the heck was going on? And why, you ask, since I was standing there feeling very much alive, do I claim that my life ended that day out on Highway 5, east of Saskatoon? Because just as I was standing there, beginning to realize I was feeling better than I'd felt in a very long time, I looked over at the mangled car and saw my equally mangled old body hanging from the seat belt.

CHAPTER TWO

Panic and confusion. Those two words pretty much sum up the next few hours of my life, but they fall short when describing the first few minutes after seeing my dead body. What the heck is going on? That's me! But I'm me! What the hell? My thoughts were bouncing around in my head and my new heart was racing so fast I was afraid I'd have a heart attack.

I ran the few steps over to the car and took a closer look at the old me. As battered as I was, and I was a mess let me tell you, it was still obviously me. Knowing that only seemed to increase my panic. If that's me, then who the heck am I? It was then that the youthful appearance of my hands finally sank in and I looked down at my new body. I was wearing blue jeans and a T-shirt and, more surprising, I was now slim and obviously very fit. I looked around to see if there was any unbroken glass on the car that I could catch my reflection in and found that all the windows were shattered. The mirrors! I reached in front of my lifeless old body and tore the mirror off the windshield. As I peered into it, the face that looked back shocked and delighted me in equal measure.

It was me. But it was the 'Me' I remembered from sixty years ago, give or take a decade. Granted, the mirror was too thin to show me my whole face at once and I had to shift it side to side to see my myself ear to ear, but it looked like me. Only it was me from the past, with a full head of hair and a wrinkle-free face. In my crazed and hyperventilating state I had the thought that this was a great new product for a shopping channel advertisement.

Do you want to regain your youthful appearance? Send us three easy payments of just forty-nine ninety-five, and we'll send out a soccer mom to run your old butt off the road! Act before this program ends and we'll include a new pair of jeans and a T-shirt.

I actually laughed out loud, and the sudden sound of my voice shocked me part way out of my panic.

Still, a dozen questions were fighting for space in my hysteria-stricken head until one concept, that I was now a young man at the scene of a fatal accident with no explanation for why I was there, forced all other thoughts from my mind. I quickly checked the pockets of my jeans and found them empty. Wonderful! I had no identification and no way to explain who I was or where I came from and what I was doing several miles out of the city.

I scrambled up onto the highway and saw a vehicle coming from the east, heading toward Saskatoon. Looking back, I could see that the totaled car was completely hidden from the highway by tall grass. I dove back down into the ditch, hoping that the driver of the vehicle hadn't noticed me. Within seconds it went speeding by and I let go of my breath in a whoosh. I hadn't realized I was holding my breath; like the truck driver might hear me breathing as he went past.

Gall-darn it, Orville, get a grip! Oh yeah! That's my name. Orville. Orville Olsen.

I had jumped back into the ditch, because I couldn't head back to the city with empty pockets. Without money I'd have nothing to eat, and if the day came to an end while I was still living this unbelievable fantasy, I'd also be needing a place to sleep. I couldn't just head back to Arbor Village and take up my life where I'd left off. How would I explain my rejuvenated state to the other residents? 'Oh, I was run off the road by a cell phone addict and woke up in this new body.' No one would believe it, and if they did, I could be trampled to death by the mad rush of excited seniors desperate to get to their vehicles.

However, I knew where I could get money. The old me always carried more cash than I ever needed. Strange. It was my money, but I felt like I was doing something very wrong when I reached in to get it.

Holy Cow, old man! That is one boney butt you've got there.

Retrieving my wallet was easy with my old rear end pointing to the sky the way it was. Getting the cash out of my front pockets was more difficult because of the seatbelt that held me suspended above the roof of the car. Fortunately, my new and improved body was strong, and I was able to push the old me up off the belt enough to free the money and then tuck the emptied pocket back in where it belonged. I didn't want it to look as though I'd been robbed when the wreck was finally discovered.

A couple hundred dollars and change. More than enough to take care of my immediate needs. My credit and debit cards would keep me going a bit longer, depending of course on how soon my body was found. How long after that would my cards be cancelled? I had no idea, but there was no time to worry about it. I had to get away from the wreck and get back to the city. I took one last look at my mangled old self.

"Goodbye, old man," I whispered.

It was best to get some distance from the wreck before

going back up on the highway to hitch a ride. Hopping over a barbed-wire fence, I walked several feet into a field of wheat and started heading toward town. How incredibly easy it was to jump that fence. Just the act of walking was an absolute pleasure! How long had it been since any movement had been a pleasure? I felt fantastic! In fact, I felt like I could possibly run the dozen or so miles back to the city. I felt like I could jump over a house!

Once again, I looked down at my new body. My arms were muscular, much more so than they'd ever been in my youth. In reality, I'd always been a bit on the pudgy side. These arms looked very strong indeed, and I flexed them, amazed at the size of both biceps. My right arm was covered in blood from when I'd availed myself of my wallet and cash, so I bent down to wipe it off on the dew-covered wheat. Noticing how wet the plants were made me check to see what was protecting my feet, and I found I was wearing a new looking pair of army style boots. I looked like any young person might look in this day and age. My clothes seemed new and relatively clean, which would be advantageous when I got back on the highway to hitch a ride.

I felt fantastic. Aside from the energy and strength that powered my every movement, I was astonished by the stabbing brilliance of the scene before me, the clarity of each sound, and probably most intense of all, the potency of every aroma. Did this new body come with augmented senses or was it just that the old me had grown accustomed to worn out tools? The meadowlarks perched on my shoulder and sang right into my ears. The greens and golds of the ripening wheat could have been squeezed from fresh tubes of artist's oil paint. The sunlight sparkling off the dew-covered plants pierced my new eyes with a nearly painful intensity. All of this inflated my chest with an inner joy that made me want to spin around with my arms outstretched and sing, "The hills are alive with the sound of music".

For crying out loud, Orville, get a grip!

A few cars went by, some heading into town and some heading east. When they passed, I would squat down to hide in the tall crops. After walking a half mile or so I had put a couple of hills between me and the wreck and decided it was time to get back on the highway. I hopped over another wire fence and climbed back up onto the road.

The first two cars that went by didn't even slow down, and the third driver braked and slowed as she went by and then hit the gas again. Did I appear threatening in some way? The fourth vehicle was a big Dodge 4x4, and he hit the binders as soon as he saw me, and I gave him a wave as he rolled past. I didn't want to look too eager, don't ask me why, so I jogged slowly up to the truck. The driver, a man in his mid-forties, had the door unlatched when I got there.

"Where ya headed?" The compulsion to say that when you pick up a hitchhiker must be overwhelming. Everyone does.

"Saskatoon," I replied.

"What the hell are you doing out here?"

"Girlfriend and I had a fight. She kicked me out of the car."

"And you got out?" he laughed. "You must really like walking!"

"Like it better than I like her right now," I said.

He laughed again as he pulled away from the side of the road.

"Mike Friesen," he said.

"Orville." It was out of my mouth before I realized it.

"Ya don't hear that name much anymore," he said. "Especially on someone your age."

"It was my grandfather's name, and I guess my parents liked it. Where you headed?" I asked, wanting to get him talking before I started losing track of my lies.

"Saskatoon. Coming back from Yorkton. Just finished up a job there last night, but it was too late, and I was too tired."

Thank God I got a driver who liked to talk. He went on

11

and on about I'm not sure what, and every once and a while he would look at me for a response, so I'd say "Oh yeah" or "Uh-huh" and he'd be off again. I didn't mean to be rude, but I was still so gob-smacked by my rebirth that I could only listen to my own thoughts. *What the hell is going on? How can I still be alive? Why am I young?* That was it, really. Those three questions just kept bouncing around in my head. Eventually, though, another one added itself to the first three. *What the heck am I going to do?*

After learning that it was not much out of Mike's way, I had him drop me off at the Circle Centre Mall on 8th Street. It was a place where I could find a bank or two, and I wanted to withdraw as much money as I could over the next couple of days. Also, there were several places to eat. I was famished. When had this body eaten last? For that matter, had this body ever eaten before?

I practically ran into the food court and up to the A&W counter. I'd no sooner ordered a Grandpa Burger, fries and a large root beer when it hit me that there were mirrors in the washroom nearby. I paid the clerk, and pointing toward the restroom, asked him to hang on to my food until I got back.

Well, I have to say, I looked bloody fantastic! I'm not bragging you understand, but I looked really good. I couldn't tell for sure how tall I was, but I seemed to be about the same six-foot-one I'd been in my youth. But unlike the slightly chubby and distinctly un-athletic look I'd lived with most of my original life, this was the body of a star athlete. I lifted my T-shirt and was delighted to see stomach muscles where I'd always found flab in the past. I raised my arms into the classic double bicep pose just as another young guy walked into the washroom. Embarrassed, I dropped them again and tried to look nonchalant, but he rolled his eyes as he went past, and I'm pretty sure I heard him mumble "Loser" just as his bathroom stall latched shut. I could have stood there and stared at myself all day, but I didn't want to be there when the guy came back out. Besides, I really was hungry, so I washed my hands and went out to get my food.

It probably goes without saying that the food tasted amazing. Was it enhanced senses, overwhelming hunger or just the contrast to the old, worn out taste buds I was accustomed to? I couldn't tell you, but that hamburger made me feel like everything was going to be okay. Mind you, I'd always been that way. If I ever started to get grumpy or if I was starting to worry about something, even something worth worrying about, all I needed was a full stomach and everything seemed alright. I don't really like to admit it, but it was one of the things that made me miss my Elsie the most. She always knew when I needed to be fed. I was suddenly filled with the same intense feeling of loneliness that I always felt when thinking of my late wife, and it sat very strangely in this new body, having to share space with other emotions like excitement, hysteria, awe and confusion. However, now that my stomach was full, I was beginning to lose the sense of panic that had been with me since waking up next to my old, mangled self.

Though the food court in a busy shopping centre might not be the best place to do it, it was time to take stock of my situation and make some decisions about what I was going to do. It seemed pointless to focus on questions I didn't have an answer for. Instead, I decided to look at what I did know and use that information to help plan my next few steps. I was alive. Well, okay, maybe I was actually dead and experiencing a very strange purgatory, but for practical purposes, I was alive. I was rejuvenated, young, and very fit. How this happened was beyond my comprehension, but it was nonetheless so. My old body was dead and hanging in a wrecked car a few miles outside of the city, and would no doubt be discovered at some point in the near future. I had some money, and my credit and debit cards would give me access to a bit more, provided I used them before my old body was discovered. A small amount of panic returned, and I decided to forgo any further ruminations in favour of finding a bank machine.

At the Scotiabank in the east end of the mall, I was able to withdraw five thousand from savings with the debit card and five thousand from my Visa. I may have been able to get more, but I didn't want to exceed my daily limits on either card. For all I knew, that would raise a flag somewhere, and I would lose access to my money entirely. If I waited until tomorrow, I could withdraw another ten-thousand dollars, and after that, I would have to check the papers to see if the wreck had been found or if anyone had noticed I was missing. Either event would likely result in my bank accounts and credit cards being frozen.

Feeling better about having more cash in my pocket, I bought a coffee and again took a seat in the food court to spend more time planning my immediate future.

I had identification in my wallet, but if I was ever asked, I'd be better off having none to show, than to connect myself with a ninety-one-year-old man lying dead in a ditch. I resolved to dispose of my wallet. However, I had already made mistakes. Giving my real first name, a name that no one my apparent age would be likely to have, to the man that picked me up on the highway was not a brilliant thing to do. If he ever heard news of an old man named Orville being killed on the same road, he might be inspired to share his story with the police. He would describe an athletic young man in a white T-shirt and jeans whose name also happened to be Orville. Was the hitchhiker going by that name because that was the one on the identification he had stolen? I had to stop using my real name. I needed to take steps to disassociate my new self from my former self. At the very least I should go shopping and by myself a different shirt.

I couldn't go home or contact anyone who knew me. No one would believe I was who I claimed to be. Also, making such a claim would likely result in a visit to a psych ward. I may have thought I was a lonely old man in my former life, but in this life, I really was truly alone.

'Can you believe the fine mess I've gotten myself into, Elsie?' I asked the ghost that was ever present in my mind.

'It seems to me you've been given a second chance, Orville. You should probably make the most of it.'

In my imagination, I knew what my always practical late wife would tell me. She would advise me to stop looking for problems and put my advantages to work. It was one of the reasons we were such a good partnership for so many years. Each of us knew when the other needed support.

One of the running jokes that my wife and I had enjoyed for many years was my pathetic impressions of Laurel and Hardy, a comedy team from the days of black and white movies. Oliver Hardy was a pompous bully who mistreated the smaller childlike Stan Laurel. Despite being the apparent leader of the pair, Hardy was always blaming Laurel for all the trouble the two found themselves in. "This is another fine mess you've gotten us in," he would say. Laurel's inevitable reply was a silent, blinking look of guilty resignation. My attempts to mimic Stan Laurel in this signature expression always won me a giggle or a laugh from my Elsie. *Would she be amused by this mess?* I wondered.

By the end of the day, I was going to need a place to sleep. The money in my pocket would get me a hotel room for a few nights, and that would help me to feel grounded in this mess that I found myself in. I resolved that I would head out in search of a place I could call home, at least for a while. With that decision made, I stood up from my table and, turning, had my second collision of the day.

CHAPTER THREE

There was a brilliant flash of white light, and I was no longer inside a shopping centre, but outside in a parking lot. I wasn't alone, and I was talking.

"Give me the fucking backpack kid," I said.

"Fuck you, Asshole!"

"Mouthy little fucker, aren't you?" I said. I didn't seem to have any control over what I was saying. *What the heck is going on? I thought.* "Hand it over! Now!" I said.

The kid I was threatening looked to be a boy of about twelve or thirteen. He was dressed in jeans and a hooded top and was carrying a black knapsack slung over one shoulder. Behind him was an older skinny kid with a constellation of pimples and a creepy smile on his face. Without intending to, I felt myself stepping forward and swinging my right arm toward the younger child. To my horror, my right hand held a knife.

***

Suddenly, there was another white flash, and I found myself back in the food court. I was facing another young guy of about sixteen or so as he was getting up off the floor.

"Fucking Asshole!" he said to me.

I stared at him dumbly for several seconds as I determined that, upon rising from the table and turning, I had run into him as he was walking past. The impact must have knocked him to the ground.

"Sorry," I said, even though I didn't really feel sorry. The boy looked like a young punk to me, and I didn't appreciate being called a "Fucking Asshole" by anyone, let alone a young punk.

The young punk glared at me and deliberately slammed his shoulder into mine as he moved to go past. I wasn't really braced for it, but his assault had little effect on me. It was then that I noticed he was not alone, for also glaring at me with the same kind of threatening eyes was the skinny, acne-faced kid I had just seen in the parking lot.

I stood there stunned and watched the two of them as they shuffled away, muttering to each other. They were, in my opinion, the very picture of two teenage misfits up to no good.

I turned and sat back down in my seat, and for the second time in one day, unchecked thoughts began bouncing around in my head. *What the heck is going on? What was that? Am I going nuts now?* I had to forcibly slow both my thoughts and my breathing as I tried to get a grip on what had just happened.

As the panic began to subside, it dawned on me that I must have had some sort of vision brought on by my contact with that young punk. In the vision, young Acne Boy had seemed to be acting as my accomplice in the attempted robbery of a younger kid. If that were so, then I must have been seeing this strange vision through the eyes of the teen with whom I had

17

had the collision. It was as if I was temporarily looking at the world from his eyes and watching myself, as him, threatening to steal a younger boys bag. The thought of these two creepy little buggers forcing their will on anyone suddenly made me very angry and, without thinking, I found myself getting up from the table and turning to follow them. I had no way of knowing if what I had experienced was a vision of something that had really happened or if it was anything more than my imagination, but I felt very strongly that I shouldn't let the two of them out of my sight.

The Circle Centre Mall had initially been two smaller shopping centres that were expanded and connected a few decades back. A tunnel had been built under Acadia Street to join the food court in the west half of the mall to the movie theatres in the east. By the time I began following them, the two young creeps had already descended into this walkway, but I spotted them as soon as I rounded a bend in the corridor. I walked at a pace just fast enough to keep them in sight. I didn't want to catch up to them until I decided what I was going to do. I couldn't exactly accost them and demand to know if they had stolen a bag from a younger boy. Or, could I? As I was walking, and trying desperately to decide what I should do, I noticed that they were also following someone.

Holy Cow! I thought.

It was the young boy from my vision. The shock stopped me dead in my tracks as my brain again began to race out of control.

Get a grip, you bozo! I told myself.

I needed to stop letting my mind go into panic mode every time some strange new thing happened to me. Obviously, strange new things were becoming the norm.

It's going to happen! They're going to rob that kid! I started walking again picking up my pace.

They turned down a small exit corridor by Scotiabank, and without giving it any thought, I followed them out into the parking lot. All I could do was make it up as I went along. I just knew that I wasn't going to let those two little buggers harm that young boy.

"Hand it over! Now!"

Holy Cow! It's just like my vision! Only now, instead of being in front of the younger boy and holding a knife, I was behind the creep who was in front of the boy, and he had the knife.

"Why don't you two pick on someone your own size?" *Crap!* I thought. *Couldn't I have been more original than that?*

The guy was starting his knife swing at the younger boy. He checked himself and spun to face me. Startled by my size and proximity, he took a quick step backward, almost into the boy with the backpack. His expression went from confident belligerence to surprise, and then to one of desperate defensiveness. He held the knife in front of him like it was a shield instead of a weapon. He seemed no better prepared for this encounter than I was. I was okay with that.

"Why don't you mind your own business, Fuck Head?"

Okay, so his lines weren't going to be very original either. He took a quick look behind him to see where his buddy was, and Acne Boy stepped forward hesitantly like he'd rather have been somewhere else.

"Put the knife away and get the heck out of here and maybe you two won't get your butts kicked!"

I don't even know why I was acting so aggressive. I guess I was still on a bit of a high after seeing how fit and young I'd become. It might have been smarter to check if this new body had come with any combat skills before I started picking fights with armed street thugs.

"I'll cut you, Fucker!"

The creep jabbed the knife forward, but not even close to where I was in danger of being stabbed. I noticed that the younger boy had run over to a bus stop shelter and turned back to watch the proceedings. Taking advantage of my momentary distraction, the punk swung the knife again, determined to do me harm this time, but he did it so slowly that I easily stepped back out of range. Having missed with the first swing, he stepped forward with the backswing, intent on drawing blood. But he moved so slowly!

This kid has got to be on drugs, I thought.

I was able to get my abdomen, his intended target, out of the way again by jackknifing my body and going up on my toes. As his knife hand swung past me the second time, I reached out and grabbed his wrist, something I wouldn't have dared to do if it were not for him moving like he was swimming in molasses. Once I had him, I squeezed, pulled and twisted all at once in a desperate effort to make him release the knife. He screamed and slammed into me, more the result of my having pulled him off balance than through any intent of his own, but fortunately dropped the blade at the same time. I stumbled backward a little but managed to quickly regain my footing. He was now slightly bent forward so I did the first thing that came to mind and punched down at him, shifting my aim at the last moment to smash him in the back of the shoulder rather than his head. Good thing, as the force of the blow drove him to the pavement like he'd had a piano dropped on him.

I looked up from him expecting to ward off an attack from his friend, but his backup had backed up and was turning to make an escape. I watched as he ran right past the younger boy and kept on running until he was out of sight.

The young boy was staring at me like a deer caught in headlights. Obviously, he couldn't believe I had come to his rescue. Fearing I had done serious harm to the creep on the ground I looked down, just as he moaned and mumbled something unintelligible. He was probably going to live. I quickly scanned the area to see if anyone else had witnessed the encounter and, seeing only the young boy I had saved, concluded my good deed would likely go unpunished. I nodded to the lad, who continued to stare like I was a circus freak, and headed back into the building.

Once again my mind was going hyperactive. I needed to

find a place where I could be alone with my thoughts. But first I needed to get away from this mall, as I didn't know for sure that my little fight hadn't been witnessed or that the punk I fought wouldn't call security on me, ironic as that might be. It now seemed even more critical that I pick up a change of clothes. I walked straight through the mall, out the front doors, and headed west.

CHAPTER FOUR

Eighth Street is one of Saskatoon's business and retail districts, housing office buildings, stores and restaurants along most of its roughly seven-kilometre span. The last time I looked, and admittedly that could well have been many years ago, there was a motel several blocks to the west and, if memory served, about halfway there, there should be a Winner's store where I could pick up some new clothes. It was a hike that would have been out of the question in my old body. Now, however, I felt that I could effortlessly run the full distance, and part of me wanted to try. With every step I took, I could feel the muscles in my thighs flexing, and it made me wonder what the limits of this new body might be. I felt like I had no physical limits whatsoever. In contrast to the last few years of my life, when any trip of more than a few steps had to be planned out in advance to ensure that there would be places to rest along the way, just being able to set off in any direction with absolute certainty that I could get where I was going was like having a superpower. *Stay tuned to this channel for the amazing adventures of Young Orville! Faster than a drugged-out street thug! Able to walk vast distances in a single day!* OK. Maybe not a superpower, but beyond the dreams of the average ninety-one-year-old.

As a boy, I was a bookworm. These days they're are called nerds. Bookworms, in my day, were not interested in sports, avoided most things physical and spent their days reading. Nerds, to my understanding, are not interested in sports, avoid most things physical and spend their days playing video games, watching TV or reading. The significant difference in the generations is that bookworms were looked down on by most others and were often challenged to find their place in the world. The nerds of today, on the other hand, rule the world. I couldn't help but smile thinking that now when being a young nerd would be a positive thing, I find myself in the body of a young athlete. Oh well, not so bad. There are star athletes out there who make more money than the leaders of most nations.

Holy crap! What am I going to do? I thought. *Am I really going to have to start over? How the heck am I going to find my way? How will I fit in? How will I earn a living?* Funny. Those are the same kind of questions I often asked myself seventy years ago.

I began to wonder how old this body was, or rather, how old it appeared to be. As I had grown older, I found it increasingly difficult to judge the ages of young people. By the time I was in my eighties I couldn't say for sure if a young person was eighteen or thirty, young women especially. Makeup didn't help any. Now I'm in the unique situation of being unable to determine my own apparent age. At some point, I'll have to get some new identification. What the heck age am I going to put on my driver's license?

I pulled my wallet out of my back pocket. I opened it as I walked along and looked at the small tokens of my life that I kept there. My driver's license picture made me shiver. That was a picture of me! The real me! That was the man that had built a life in this little city, had married a young woman who would become his best friend, had two healthy children and watched them grow up to have families of their own. That was me, not this young man with these muscles and this thick head of hair.

What the heck is going on?

Looking at these remnants of my former life, all that I now had left of that life, was making me feel very, very lonely. But underlying every feeling I'd had since the time of my rebirth was a subtle but ever-present loneliness. The panic, confusion, and excitement that I'd experienced in varying degrees and combinations every thirteen seconds or so for the past few hours were new to me. But the loneliness? That was left over from the original me. That older me recognized that feeling. Sure, I had had family around me. In that way as well, I was much more fortunate than many other people my age. But even with family around, and despite getting along quite well with many of the other people in the senior's complex, despite never spending too much time alone, I had become very, very lonely. It wasn't just due to the loss of my wife of six decades. All of my friends and associates were gone. All of my contemporaries had passed. I had grown so tired of losing people close to me that, a decade or so ago, I stopped getting close to anyone. The only exception was my great-granddaughter, Jenny. That kid had somehow wormed her way into my life and my heart. She was the only one in my old life that I felt a strong emotional connection to, and now, knowing that I had lost her too, made the loneliness even more intense.

I wiggled the tips of my thumb and forefinger into the most recessed slot in the old wallet and carefully removed the picture of my late wife, Elsie. It was the only picture I had ever kept there. Taken when she was in her early thirties, it was my favourite picture of her. She'd been looking at the camera with the look she often gave me, a look of mild incredulity. That look was often accompanied by a questioning "Really?", like she couldn't quite believe I'd said what I'd just said. God, I missed her! I noticed with a strange comfort that the hollow, empty pain I experienced every time I thought of her felt exactly the same in this new chest as it had in the old one.

I wanted to hang on to the credit and debit cards that I used earlier, but I knew that any of these cards and pieces of identification would only cause problems if someone ever found them in my possession. After all, they belonged to a dead man in a ditch. I placed the picture between the two bank cards I still needed and considered disposing of the wallet with the rest of its contents. Where could I dispose of a wallet? A block south of Eighth Street there were several small apartment buildings that would have dumpsters behind them, but I didn't think I should toss the wallet into one of them. I'd often seen street people - *when did we stop calling them Bums?* - digging through those dumpsters in search of treasure. I didn't want one of them to have the find-of-the-week and do something that would result in my bank accounts becoming inaccessible to me. I'd have to hang on to my wallet and wait for a better opportunity to dispose of it.

Eighth street is a pretty busy place on a sunny Sunday afternoon and today was no exception. With all of the people rushing about I should have felt fairly anonymous, just one more guy on the active city street, but I didn't. I was aware of a nagging feeling that I was being watched. Was I just being paranoid, worried I might be implicated in the death of an old man or the beating of a young hooligan? Or was I just self-conscious walking the street in a new, very young, very fit body? No one could tell by looking at me that this body wasn't mine. There's no law against having a new body, anyway. But it was a body that would attract the notice of many people, just because of how it looked in tight jeans and a T-shirt. Looking into the oncoming cars as they passed, I found many of the occupants were looking back. A Honda Civic with its windows down and music blaring went by, and the driver honked as the three young female passengers all waved and craned their necks.

It sure is a different world! I thought, reflecting that girls of my time would never have been that forward. Just then another car, a small Lexus, went by and a male voice with a definite feminine lilt hollered out from the passenger side window, "Hey there, Sweetie!" *Yup, it really is a different world!*

In less time than I could believe I was across the street from the Winner's store and at the green light I jogged over and entered. I had no idea what size this new body would wear, so I grabbed a medium and a large in the first shirt I found and headed for the change rooms. Once inside I pulled my T-shirt off and tried on the medium, finding it fit much as my original shirt did, that being too tight for my liking. The large was roomier and didn't accent my muscles so much. I decided to buy it. Before putting my T-shirt back on I looked for a label to see if it too was a large, but it was entirely label-free. *Strange.* Checking my jeans, I found that they also had no manufacturer's label in them, but they did have a small tab with "32/34" inside. Thirty-two-inch waist and a thirty-four-inch inseam. It seemed that shopping together was a great way to get to know someone, even when that someone was yourself.

Before heading to the checkout, I found another shirt of the same style as the first but in a different colour, and a light summer jacket in an extra-large that fit quite well. I also grabbed a small gym bag and a black belt. I didn't need the belt to hold my pants up, but I'd always worn a belt, and I felt a little under-dressed without one.

Once outside, I headed into the drug store next door and picked up a toothbrush, some toothpaste, and a watch that looked pretty good for only thirteen ninety-five. I asked the lady at the checkout for the time so I could set my new watch and was surprised to learn it was only twelve forty-five. It had been an eventful morning. Outside again, I put my new belongings in my new gym bag and headed up the street to where I hoped to find a motel.

The remaining walk to the motel took me past more retail outlets, many of them undergoing minor facelifts, and a small city park consisting of a beautifully manicured lawn and a few trees. As I strolled, the mild panic and paranoia persisted.

I found the motel, named the Colonial, right where I thought it would be. A man at the desk, who seemed so bored he might drift off to sleep and fall off his stool, didn't want to give me a room if I couldn't provide a credit card. When I told him my wallet was stolen when I'd fallen asleep in the Prince Albert Bus Depot, he gave me a sour look and suggested I could pay cash for two nights stay up front. He gave me a first-floor room facing south with direct access to the parking lot.

The room was exactly like every motel room in every small motel in North America. A bed, a small desk and chair, a window to the street and a small washroom at the back. As excited as I was to get to the mirror and gawk some more at my new body, I never made it. I took one look at the bed and toppled on to it. I was unconscious before my head hit the pillow.

I awoke at five fifteen, assuming the accuracy of my fourteen-dollar watch, and was instantly wide awake. I don't think that I was physically tired at all, but rather the shock of the morning's strange events had been psychologically draining. The four hours I'd been asleep were completely dreamless and passed as if I was under anesthetic. I leapt out of bed and bounced into the washroom.

This morning, about twelve hours earlier, getting out of bed had been quite a different story. Like most mornings over the past few years, I had awoken slowly, thoughts of my late wife slowly coming into focus until the recognition of a persistent loneliness confirmed I was no longer asleep. The decision to get out of bed also happened slowly, but not nearly as slowly as the actual act. A ninety-one-year-old body at rest really wants to remain at rest. Just getting upright can take a couple of minutes and this morning it was another minute or two before I was confident that I could take a step without risking a fall. The first few steps were always painful, my knees and ankles not wanting to bend and flex the way they were designed.

Twelve hours later, the trip from the bed to the washroom happened before I was even aware I'd made the decision to move. Apparently, there was not going to be any learning curve involved in adapting to this new body. I found myself answering the call of nature as automatically as I had gotten out of bed. I won't go into a description of how this experience differed from the ninety-one-year-old equivalent, but trust me, everything about being in a younger, healthier, stronger body was better than being old. Everything.

I removed my clothes and stepped into the shower. I'd always loved a good hot shower and, having spent part of the morning walking through farmers' fields, I felt I could use a little washing up. I don't think any shower I'd taken since my early teens had been so preoccupied with self-exploration. I felt and flexed every part of my new self that I could possibly feel and flex, and again marvelled at how robust this new me was. I ran my hands over my torso and squeezed my shoulder-blades together, feeling the muscles bunch. As I spread soap over my body, I ran my hands down over my thighs and bent to rub my bulging calf muscles and even applied soap to my toes. My toes and I hadn't been close in recent years and being able to easily grab them like this, simply by bending at the waist, was another reminder that this was a much fitter version of my younger self than the original. I felt so exuberant that, on a whim, I shut off the hot water and rinsed myself off with the water as cold as it would get. It's called a "James Bond Shower", first as hot as is bearable and then as cold as the water will run. I had tried it a few times many years earlier. Back then I found it invigorating, but I never learned to love the experience. Today, many years later and six or seven decades younger, it made me feel like a god.

Exiting the shower, I toweled myself off in front of the mirror and again tried to determine just how old this body might be. I guessed that I looked to be in about my mid-twenties, but I really wasn't sure. As lean as I was, I could be in my late teens, but my face looked a little more mature than that. As I was pondering it, my stomach growled and I realized I was hungry again, so I quickly got dressed and stepped outside to search for a place to eat.

The motel, it turned out, had its own pub and grill, so I strode boldly in, hoping I at least looked old enough to order a drink. A pretty, young lady behind the bar told me to sit anywhere, so I picked a table in a back corner where I felt I'd have some privacy. As I sat, I watched as another young lady, the waitress, unloaded a tray of glasses at the bar, and the two girls looked over at me and spoke to each other a bit, smiling and laughing. The waitress then headed my way, and I was sure she was about to ask me for ID, but when she got to the table she greeted me with the traditional "What can I get you?" and I slowly let out my breath before asking for a Great Western Light and a menu. As she walked back to the bar, I immediately forgot my worries about my age and enjoyed the movement of her backside in her remarkably snug jeans.

I barely had time to consider how long it had been since I'd last enjoyed the sight of a girl in blue jeans when she was on her way back to my table with a menu. She was quite a beautiful young woman. I must have been very distracted not to have noticed it right off the bat. Smiling, she leaned down to place the menu and a coaster on the table in front of me, exposing a considerable amount of cleavage.

"Your beer will be right up," she said, and as I glanced from her smile to the creamy smooth skin of her chest, I detected a reaction inside my own snug jeans.

Oh my Christ! I thought. *I'm a teenager!*

"Are you okay?" asked the waitress.

Obviously, some of what I was thinking was registering on my face.

"Uh, yeah, uh, I'm fine. I just realized I forgot something I had to do. Sorry!"

"No worries! I'll be right back."

I couldn't believe It. One glance at a pair of breasts and I start to get a Woodie! I must be very young indeed! It's not that in my old age I had stopped getting erections, but I learned how not to get them at inappropriate times all the way back when I was in grade school. I had to admit, though, that I was rather tickled at the thought that that part of my life might be rejuvenated as well. On the other matter, the waitress hadn't given any indication that I might be under bar age, so I was feeling confident that my assessment of a mid-twenties appearance was reasonably accurate.

"Here you go." The waitress was back with my beer, and I forced myself to look her in the face as she set it down. I was smiling at her rather foolishly, so I recovered my composure by asking her name.

"Demi," she said as she thrust half of her cleavage at me to draw my attention to her nametag. How could I have missed that? Never mind. I know how I missed it. Was I sweating? "What's yours?"

"Orville," I replied. Again, it was out of my mouth before I'd given it any thought.

"Orville! Wow! You don't hear that name very often. I think I had a great uncle named Orville."

"Yeah, I get that reaction a lot. I was named after my grandfather." I had to stop giving my real name.

"Okay, Orville. I'll give you a minute to look at the menu." She headed off to another table.

The bar was pretty quiet, only a half dozen tables occupied and one guy at the bar. Three women that were sitting at one of the tables were glancing my way quite often. They all looked to be in their mid-forties, and something in the way they interacted told me they'd been drinking for a while. Two of them were quite heavy, and the third looked like she spent half her life in a gymnasium and the other half in the sun. I tried to ignore their attention while I scanned the menu and decided what I'd have.

I put the menu down and watched Demi, who was leaving the table where the three women sat and was heading toward me.

"Have you decided? she asked.

"Beef-Dip, fries, gravy," I responded.

"The ladies over there want to know if they can buy you a beer."

Crap! I thought. *Ninety-one years old and I'm about to be hit on by a bunch of cougars.*

"I'd really rather they didn't," I told her.

"Well, are you planning on sticking around for a while?" she asked.

"Not really. Why?"

"Then you should let them buy you one. Then you can say thanks and leave after your meal. If I tell them you said no they'll be pissed."

"Okay, but take your time getting the drink to me. Okay?"

"Sure thing." Demi gave me another big smile and headed off to put in my order. I watched her walk away. Did I mention the young lady was very nicely built?

As I waited for my meal and tried to ignore the salivating predators across the room, I gave some more thought to my unusual situation. No amount of pondering was going to provide an explanation as to how I could die and rise again in another body. If such a thing had ever happened to anyone else, he or she had kept it to him or herself. A couple of thousand years ago some guy had risen from the grave, in his original body I think, and he got a lot more attention than I would ever be comfortable with, so I resolved to keep my story to myself.

I wondered if the switch would be permanent, or if this new body was a temporary thing. But all bodies are temporary, and no one knows how long theirs will last. In my original body, as old as it was, I didn't give much thought to the end.

For some reason, I'd been given another chance at life in a new one, and I'd be darned if I'd waste any more time worrying about how long it would last.

Demi arrived with my meal and another beer and, setting it down, told me it was "Compliments of the ladies over there," turning and pointing at the three women. I picked up the beer and holding it out to them I mouthed a "Thank you" and took a drink.

"Thanks, Demi."

"No problem. I'll tell them to let you eat your meal in peace."

"Appreciated."

"My pleasure, Orrr-ville," Demi teased before walking away with a big grin on her face. I don't know if she was more amused by my name or by my discomfort at the unwanted attention.

The food was good, and I ate quickly, glancing over at the table of women a couple of times as I sipped some beer. Each time I got the impression they were coiled like rattlesnakes waiting to spring. A shiver ran down my spine that made my shoulders shake and I wondered if that slight shudder was visible from across the room.

I finished my meal, downed the last of the second beer, and rose from the table all in one motion. My timing was excellent, as I met Demi at the bar and settled the tab with my back to the ladies. I said a "Good Evening" to my waitress, cutting her off as she asked about my plans for the rest of the night, and turning to the ladies, nodded and sprinted for the door. Okay, I didn't really sprint, but in my mind, I was running for my life. I couldn't quite believe it, but I was actually afraid of three middle-aged women. What the heck was my new life coming to?

CHAPTER FIVE

What to do next? It was a beautiful evening, and I didn't want to spend it hiding in my motel room, so I wandered across the street to a small park and sat down under a tree. This was the perfect place to relax and collect my thoughts.

The sun had begun its descent and as the shadows began to lengthen, the light shifted slowly to twilight red and cast a golden glow on the trees in the park and along the street. The traffic on the street was still heavy, and the sidewalks were now populated with local residents out for their evening walks. My heart was suddenly flooded with a profound happiness and gratitude. It was great to be alive!

I had never been a religious person, but I had always been grateful for what could only be called the "Blessings" in my life. Though not an exciting life by most standards, mine had been a mostly happy and healthy one, and I was always aware that I was more "Blessed" that many others. Sitting here now, enjoying this gorgeous setting in this new, healthy young body, I knew I had been granted a blessing far beyond anything I'd ever dreamed of, and the wonder and gratefulness I experienced was almost spiritual.

Young, healthy and with possibly many years before me, my gratitude was tainted with a bit of trepidation. What was I going to do? I was well aware that the world had changed a great deal since I was last a young adult. I had often commented over the years, as had many others of my generation, that I wouldn't want to be a young person in this day and age. And now here I was, a young person in this day and age. And unlike other young people, my education was not a recent one. Nor had I been moulded by today's society. I had watched as technology appeared to go crazy, as communication and entertainment became available to everyone everywhere instantaneously, and as toddlers, who had not yet mastered walking, developed skills with computers and cellphones that I believed I would never need and had never bothered to acquire. I had spent the last few decades on the sidelines, never thinking I would ever again be asked to take the field.

On the other hand, nine decades had taught me things that only time and experience can bestow. Unlike most young people of any era, I knew that the doubts and fears that feel unique to each of us are experienced, though seldom shared, by all of us. I knew that the challenges that overwhelm us today are most often insignificant memories after the passage of but a few days. And I knew in a way that only the elderly know, that it is the people we gather around us that have genuine value and that it is those connections that we miss the most when they are gone. I was hit once again with another intense pang of loneliness.

'Oh, Elsie! How can I still miss you so much after all this time?'

How could I have gone from gratefully enjoying a beautiful

summer evening to mourning a long-dead wife in a few short minutes of contemplation? Chalk it up to "Old habits die hard." In my case, quite old habits indeed. For several years now, I'd been in the habit of letting every thought I had lead, inevitably, to self-pity over the loss of my wife. What began many years ago as a normal, healthy mourning period had developed into a habit of thought that was quite unhealthy, the result of a decision I had made to spend the remainder of my life alone. My children and grandchildren had frequently suggested that I find a new companion with whom to share my "Declining Years". I believed that the benefits of having someone else in my life would not outweigh the challenges of adjusting to the habits and idiosyncrasies of a new partner. Of course, I had no idea that I was going to hang around into my nineties. After several years spent mostly alone with my thoughts, I had gotten into the habit of letting those thoughts drift inexorably toward memories of my dead Elsie. All of this moping around had turned me into what we used to call a "Cantankerous Old Coot." I wasn't close to anyone, except for my great-granddaughter Jenny. I knew that the other residents in the senior's complex where I lived - used to live - didn't particularly like me. They didn't necessarily dislike me either, but I made no effort to get to know them and didn't respond well when others tried to get to know me. Now it turns out that this reclusiveness was good, not just because it left fewer people to mourn my death, but also because it left me with no urge to seek out anyone from my previous life, perhaps with the exception, again, of my great-granddaughter, Jenny.

Jenny was a very sensitive young girl who might have been the only person in my life that perceived how incredibly lonely I actually was. While I saw most of my family only on holidays like Christmas and Easter, Jenny made a habit of calling once or twice a week to say hello, ask how I was doing or if I needed anything. She also ensured that we got together a couple of times a month, stopping by my place or arranging to meet somewhere for lunch. She really was a very sweet child, and I was going to miss her a great deal. I realized that I had already subconsciously decided that I would not attempt to contact her. I would not go looking for a young woman who wouldn't recognize me and who had nothing to benefit by getting involved with me.

So, what was a miserable old grump like me going to do with a second chance at life? There was no point in my trying to find out how or why I found myself reborn. The fact is, no one knows how or why any of us are here. Science may have begun to answer the question of our existence, of life's existence, but any scientist will admit they've only begun to scratch the surface of that great mystery. Most religions claim to have the answers and will share them with you in exchange for ten percent of your annual income, but it has always seemed to me that their answers only manage to raise a never-ending circle of new questions. If all the deep thinkers throughout history have failed to agree on how we came into existence, or why any of us are here, the only thing for me to do was to leave the pondering of those big questions to them and to move forward with my new life. Possibly someday a clue to the mystery of my rebirth may drop in my lap, but until that happens, I wouldn't know where to even start looking for answers.

I no longer felt my earlier panic. A long nap and a good meal had reset my emotional equilibrium, and I felt ready to take on the world. I had roughly ten thousand dollars cash, and if I was lucky, I might be able to access more before news of my death was recognized by the banking system. But, while money like that could keep me going for a year or more when I was in my twenties, today that wouldn't last much more than two or three months. Finding a job was something I'd have to look into within the next few days. And though I've never minded staying in hotels, I can't live in one forever, so finding a place to live was second on my list.

It was about this time in my musings that I became aware of a nagging sense of being watched. This wasn't the general paranoia that I suffered earlier, but rather that distinct prickling feeling at the back of the neck that one gets when being watched. Glancing around I found that I was not the only person sitting under a tree in this little park. Sitting a few yards away and facing in my direction was the young boy I'd defended at the mall. As quickly as he'd been spotted, he jumped to his feet and made to get lost.

"Hey!" I shouted.

The boy paused mid-stride, actually balanced on one foot as he decided whether to run away or not and then slowly turned and walked toward me, eyes downcast.

"It's you!" I said, the disbelief I felt edging my voice. "What are you doing here?"

"Nothing," the boy replied.

It was immediately apparent that I would be carrying this conversation.

"Have you been following me?" I asked

"I guess."

Yep, definitely carrying the conversation, so I asked, "What do you want?"

"I don't know. I guess I wanted to thank you for helping me." His response was slow, like he wasn't in the habit of thanking anyone, and it made him uncomfortable.

"You're welcome. That jerk deserved what I gave him."

At that the young boy suddenly looked up into my eyes, his face becoming quite a bit more animated as he blurted out, "That was amazing! I couldn't believe you did that! I've never seen anyone move that fast!"

As quickly as the excitement had appeared, the boy became red in the face and looked back down at the ground.

"Well, pull up some grass," I said, indicating the ground in front of me. I had risen as the lad approached me and I now sat back down and leaned back against the tree. "What's your name?"

"Aaron," the boy replied. He hesitated but finally moved to

sit as invited.

"You live around here?"

"Kind of."

"Kind of?" I repeated. We were back to dragging responses out of the kid. "You know, conversations work better if both people put in a little effort."

I was surprised to receive what could only be called a withering look from the young lad. The same look my daughter used to give me when I told her something she felt she already knew.

"I don't really live anywhere right now?"

That's better, I thought. "Well then, where are you from?"

"P.A."

Prince Albert is a small city a couple of hours drive North East of Saskatoon.

"You are quite a long way from home. Did you run away?"

"Kind of."

You are really not trying, kid! I reminded myself that most young boys go through a period of conversational deficiency at about this age.

"How old are you?" I asked.

The boy didn't respond, he just stared at the ground in front of him. Then looking up he asked, "What's your name?"

"Orville."

"Orville? You're kidding?"

"What's wrong with Orville? It was my grandfather's name."

"He should have kept it."

"Very funny. I think I liked you better when you were less talkative. Why'd you leave home?"

The lad seemed to contemplate whether or not to answer and then said, "My stepfather is an ass-hole."

"Where do you sleep?"

"Places."

Wow. I'm getting tired here. "I've got a room across the street with two beds. You're welcome to use one of them for tonight."

Aaron stared at the ground for an awkwardly long time before finally responding.

"Okay."

We sat in silence for a while before Aaron moved to the tree and sat with his back against it to the right of where I rested.

"Why'd you help me?" Aaron asked.

"I've never liked bullies," I said. "And it was obvious he was trying to steal your bag, and that would have been wrong."

"Lots of wrong shit happens. Nobody else ever does anything about it."

"You talk a bit rough for someone your age, don't you think?" I asked.

"You talk like some kind of hillbilly, don't you think?"

I hate kids!

The boy had a point, though. A person learns their manner of speech at a very young age, and unless they are forced out of it, by moving to another country where the local accent is distinctly different, or something of the sort, they never really change the way they talk. In fact, when a person moves to a new country as an adult, they often retain something of their accent for the rest of their lives. I learned my habits of speech a century ago, and in this day and age, they seem perfectly normal for someone in his nineties. But my expressions and the way I express them must seem quite unusual when voiced by someone who looked as young as I did now.

"I was raised on a farm and was mostly home-schooled. I guess I talk pretty much like my parents did," I finally replied.

"Didn't you have any friends?"

I was about to answer, "Just the farm animals." then thought better of it. That would have been asking for more trouble with this kid. Instead, I responded with something reflecting his own sullenly flippant demeanour.

"Guess not."

We sat in silence for a while. Most people aren't good with silence. They want to fill every moment with conversation whether they have anything to say or not. Aaron wasn't like that. He seemed perfectly comfortable sitting silently and waiting until a thought worth expressing came along. I left the ball in his court to see if he would make an effort to keep the conversation going.

"Where was the farm?" he asked after a bit.

"South of Yorkton. We grew mostly wheat and canola. My parents were killed in a car accident. Now it's my uncle's farm, and we don't get along, so here I am. I'd just hitchhiked into town an hour or so before I ran into you and your friends."

I have to say that starting your life over with no connections to your past really frees up your options when it comes to lying. Funny thing is, the story I made up about my parents' death actually made me feel sad. I probably have gone nuts.

"What ya gunna do?"

"Find a job and a place to live," I responded. "What are you going to do?"

Aaron had the skills of a politician when it came to ignoring questions he didn't want to answer.

"They're rebuilding the Broadway Bridge. You could probably get a job there."

That seemed like a good idea.

"That's a good idea," I said. "In fact, I like it so much, I think I'll head down there tomorrow morning."

We sat for a while watching the traffic and soon the sun was dropping out of sight in the west. I might have sat there longer and enjoyed the warm night air, but it was getting late and Aaron looked tired, so I suggested we head over to the motel and get some sleep.

Opening the door to the room, Aaron squeezed past me and headed straight into the bathroom, where he closed and locked the door. Not long after I heard the shower start. While the lad showered, I turned on the TV and watched the news. There was mention of a nasty accident on Circle Drive earlier in the day but none of a car in the ditch on Highway 5 and nothing of an old man failing to return to his retirement village. Nobody had found me, and nobody missed me, and that was totally fine by me. The longer it took for me to be found or missed, the longer I had to take money out of my bank accounts. The water stopped running just before the South Saskatchewan River ran dry. I've always liked a long hot shower, but his lad broke my longest record by several minutes. A lot of young boys have to be forced to take a shower. It must have been Aaron's first opportunity to have one in quite a long while.

The bathroom door opened, and Aaron exited, fully dressed, with his bag in hand. Were it not for the dampness of his short dark hair, I would have wondered if he'd actually showered. I went in to brush my teeth, and when I came out, I found the boy sound asleep on top of the covers, fully dressed.

Odd kid, I thought.

I stripped to my undershorts and crawled into bed. Laying there, I looked down at my new body in the dim light from the window. What an astounding day it had been. I awoke this morning a feeble old man. I was ending my day young, healthy, and strong. It had been a truly miraculous day. I smiled to myself as I lay there feeling deeply grateful for everything the day had brought. I looked over at the young boy snoring softly on his bed and realized that, for the first time in almost twenty years, I didn't feel lonely.

CHAPTER SIX

Light from the partially open curtains woke me early the next morning. I was surprised to see that Aaron was already awake. I was even more surprised to find that he was reading something on a cell phone, which he'd plugged into an outlet next to his bed. It was the first time I'd seen the phone and was amazed that he had not revealed it at some point during the previous evening. There were many times we had sat for several minutes without talking, and for anyone his age to not immediately pull out his phone and start gawking at it was, in my opinion, remarkable. I decided I liked this kid.

"Good morning," I said.

"Morning."

"Those things kill people, you know." I knew that the comment didn't really make any sense, but I was amused by it.

Aaron, of course, couldn't possibly understand the humour and glanced up at me briefly with a sort of squinty look that said, "You're weird." I decided I didn't like this kid.

"Got any plans for the day?" I asked.

"Not really."

"Well, I'd like to go downtown and find a bank. If you'd like to join me, I'll buy you breakfast."

"Okay."

We both used the bathroom to freshen up, then headed downtown.

Walking down the street on a beautiful summer morning, listening to the birds singing, feeling the fresh morning air invigorate my new and improved body, not to mention having a second chance at life, had me so high I wanted to dance in the street. I restrained myself. I knew this new life would come with its own share of problems, but I felt prepared to face them in a way that I never had in my previous life. I'd spent the last few years of my life merely going through the motions. I did pretty much the same thing every day, partially out of routine, but also out of a belief that I had nothing to gain by trying anything new. Now I wanted to try everything new, and that felt very good indeed.

I was walking quite briskly and Aaron, with his much shorter legs, was struggling to keep up. I considered slowing down but decided that if walking fast was all the kid had to do for a free breakfast it wouldn't kill him. In fact, the exercise would be good for both of us.

Once again, the conversation was minimal, and I appreciated the fact that Aaron seemed comfortable with silence. I was enjoying the scenery and wondering if the boy had any appreciation for it at all when he suddenly pointed to the top of a telephone pole where a small hawk rested.

Smiling I said, "That is a sharp-shinned hawk. I used to think they were Kestrels until one of the other residents, uh, passengers on the bus told me what it was. Kestrels are very similar, but their colouring is much more vibrant."

Aaron was looking at me funny again, but I guess he felt it went without squinting that I was weird. I realized that it was inevitable that the more comfortable I felt around this young person, the more likely it was that I would let something of the ninety-one-year-old me slip out.

"Where'd you learn to fight?" he suddenly asked.

"Oh look, there's a bird and where'd you learn to fight? You're kind of weird yourself, you know!" I said.

Aaron giggled, and I grinned.

"I've never really been in a fight before, but I've got good reflexes, and I keep in pretty good shape."

"I'll say!" Aaron replied, a pretty mature sounding response for a young boy.

"I don't think I like fighting very much, now that I've tried it," I said.

"Probably worse if you lose," Aaron said.

Okay. I like this kid.

We had reached the river, and I was reminded of how much I loved this little city that had been my home for so many years. At this time of year, the trees and bushes along the riverbank are thick with green leaves, and the fast running river is a deep, opaque blue. From here, the top of the University Bridge, also known as the 25th Street Bridge, one looked across the river at the downtown core of the city. The perfectly picturesque view was of office buildings, old churches and upstream a bit, The Bessborough Hotel. When Elsie and I moved to Saskatoon in the early Sixties, we would often picnic across the river from The Bessborough. This morning, my memory of those days was a little less bitter and a tad more sweet than it had been for many years.

We crossed the bridge and walked along Spadina Crescent until we reached 22nd Street, then headed west. On the Corner of 22nd Street and 2nd Avenue we entered the vestibule of the Bank of Montreal and, holding my breath, I tried both of my cards again. I withdrew another five thousand from each of them. Breathing what might have been a noticeable sigh of relief we exited the bank.

"You shouldn't look up at the cameras," Aaron said.

I didn't think I did.

"Why? Are you a criminal?" I asked.

"Nope. Are you?"

I didn't answer. I did take a wallet and some cash from the body of a dead man yesterday morning. Did the act make me a criminal when the body was my own?

"Where do you want to go for breakfast?" I asked.

"We could hit one of the hotels, or maybe Starbucks," Aaron replied, pointing at a Starbucks kitty-corner from where we stood.

"I think there's a Starbucks in the Midtown Plaza," I said. "Let's go there."

We headed west again.

At Starbucks in Midtown Plaza, I ordered a breakfast sandwich for each of us and a medium black coffee. Aaron rattled off a remarkable description of the coffee he wanted. It was the most words I'd heard him use in one sentence. I paid and was handed my coffee, which was hot enough to scald, and we waited for Aaron's drink and our sandwiches. I did some quick mental calculations and decided that, if we ate all of our meals at Starbucks, my twenty thousand dollars wouldn't last much more than a week.

When we got our order, we sat at a table that, as luck would have it, had the mornings Star Phoenix on it, left behind by a previous customer. As we ate, I scanned the paper to see if there was any news of a wrecked car and a broken old body being found, but again the only accident reported was the Circle Drive one.

When I finished my meal, I glanced over at Aaron and noticed that his sandwich had vanished and most of his iced, whipped cream, whatever-it-was drink was gone. He pulled out his cell phone and began tapping away on it. I read through the want ads to see what other employment opportunities there were. Saskatoon was undergoing a little economic boom, and there were lots of jobs advertised, but I liked the idea of going to the bridge in person and asking for work. Call me old fashioned.

Finishing my coffee, I folded the paper and got up from the table.

"I think I'll head over to the bridge. Are you okay on your own?" I knew it was a stupid thing to ask as soon as I asked it and I got a look from the kid said he agreed. "Meet me back at the motel later if you want," I added.

Aaron gathered up our empty food containers, tossed them in a waste bin and headed off into the shopping centre. *Kid sure doesn't waste words,* I thought, as I turned to go in search of employment.

Approaching the Broadway Bridge, I saw signs that said: "Walker Construction" mounted to a chain link fence erected around the work site. I recognized the company name. Walker Construction signs were posted at many significant projects around the city in recent years, and the impression I had was of a well-respected company. A large gate, where a temporary road provided vehicles access to the site, was wide open and, trying to look confident, I walked in and headed toward the first guy I saw wearing a white hard hat. I hadn't taken more than five steps into the site when the guy turned and saw me. He held his hand up as he started toward me.

"You can't be in here without proper gear," he shouted.

"I'm just here looking for work," I replied, not shouting, but talking loud and still trying to project a confidence that I wasn't feeling.

"Okay," he replied, dragging out the word and making it one syllable longer than it should have been. He looked me up and down. "I'll take you to see the foreman."

He led me back outside the fence to where a trailer sat just south of the bridge on what used to be lawn. There was a large Walker Construction Sign hung on one side. Stepping inside, I found a room where safety posters covered all the walls. A guy was looking at blueprints in one corner of the main room and another guy was sitting behind a computer in an adjoining office.

"Gary, there's a guy here looking for work." White Hat Guy had held the door open for me but had only poked his head in far enough to address Gary. The door closed and he was gone, leaving me standing there not quite knowing what I should do.

After what felt like several minutes, I was about to clear my throat to get attention when Gary looked up at me over his computer and waved me into his office.

"What's your name?" Gary asked.

"Orville. Orville Olson, sir" I know. I did it again.

"Really?" Gary asked.

I didn't respond, just waited.

"Okay. What experience have you got?"

"No experience in construction sir, but I was raised on a farm. I know how to work."

"Really?" He seemed to find me mildly amusing. "Okay. Think you can handle a jackhammer?"

"Pretty sure I can, sir," I replied.

This seemed to amuse him even more. I really don't know what he was finding so amusing, and I was starting to get a little irritated.

Smiling, Garry said, "Okay. We can always use a strong back around here, and you do look strong enough. Let's get you signed up. I'll need your Social Insurance Number."

"Uh, my wallet got stolen in the bus depot yesterday. They got all of my ID," I said.

Gary put both hands on the edge of his desk and pushed himself back in his chair. The smile was gone from his face.

"I'm sorry, son, but I've had nothing but bad experiences hiring guys with no identification. You'll have to get your SIN card replaced. You can do it online these days. Come back when you've got it, and we'll put you to work. Oh, and you'll need to provide a blank cheque from your bank account to get paid."

I had just gone from feeling slightly nervous to irritated, to excited, and then disappointed, all in the span of about a minute and a half.

Gary got up from the desk and held out his hand. "Sorry, son. Best I can do."

I reached out to shake his hand, and there was a brilliant white flash!

***

I was running toward a skinny guy with a jackhammer. I was screaming at him to "Look out!" My heart was pounding with fear, but the guy with the jackhammer had headphones on, and the machine he was holding was making a deafening racket. The skinny guy was facing toward me, but his head was down and behind him, and to the right a large cube van was rolling backwards, heading right at him. It was picking up speed and was about to crush the guy against the cement barrier that was the side of the bridge.

"Barry!" I yelled, my heart thudding in my chest.

***

And then I was back and letting go of Gary's hand.

I must have looked like I was about to be hit by a truck myself, because Gary once again said, "I'm sorry, son."

"Uh, no, that's okay. I understand. Thanks. I'll be back." I turned quickly and headed out of the trailer.

Once outside I immediately scanned the worksite for a cube van like the one I'd just seen. There was no such truck to be found. There were, however, two guys working with jackhammers on the higher, South-East end of the bridge and one of them looked like he could be the skinny guy I'd seen a moment earlier.

I turned and quickly headed toward another bridge, the one called the Traffic Bridge, which was located a short distance West of this end of the worksite. The Traffic Bridge, I'd always thought of it as the Victoria Bridge, angled away from the Broadway Bridge so that it met up with Victoria Avenue on the East side of the river. Victoria Avenue was about three long blocks away from the other end of the work-site. Basically, where I needed to be was many blocks away from where I was, and I had to get there fast, because, unlike yesterday in the mall, today I knew that the flash of vision I had when I shook Gary's hand was a brief glimpse of the future. I knew it didn't make any more sense than an old man dying and waking up in a younger body. I knew that there was no way I could explain it, even if there was someone to explain it to. I also knew that I had to save the life of a man with a jackhammer, and knowing that, I broke into a run.

CHAPTER SEVEN

Despite my excitement, I tried to set a steady pace and not run as fast as I could. I'd have to run the equivalent of several long city blocks, and even in this new body, I didn't think I could run the full distance flat out. I didn't want to find myself already winded before I reached the steepest uphill part of my trek, from Victoria to Broadway on the east side of the river.

The situation was very grave. A man's life was at stake, and I had no idea how much time I had to get to the scene of what I knew would be an accident, but I still could not ignore the fact that I was enjoying myself. I was absolutely sure that I was the only one who could save this man from a horrible fate. The thought would have made my heart pound were I not running a thousand-meter race. Even if I arrived in time, it was entirely possible I might not be able to save him. Any number of things could go wrong. Yet, despite the gravity of the situation, I could not deny that I was having the time of my life. I am a pathetically self-centred individual.

Of course, I already knew that about myself. My wife, Elsie, told me I was self-centred about, let's see, probably three million times over the course of our marriage. But she still loved me, and she was a wonderful person, so I could never really bring myself to worry about it or try to change. Yes, I admit, I'm flawed.

Even at just a fast jogging pace, the ground slip beneath me at a rate I could never have hoped for in my original youth. My body soon adopted a rhythm on its own as if running was something it had always done, despite my not having run in more than thirty years. Perhaps I could have gone the entire distance at my top speed, whatever that may have been. But getting back to the worksite before the accident occurred was more important than testing my limits, so I kept a steady pace suited to distance running.

When I reached the east side of the river, I was slightly winded and new that my slower than maximum pace was the right decision. I leapt a fence separating the walkway from the paved approach, and the act was natural like this body had trained for jumping. I began making my way up the three-block stretch to Broadway Street. This was an uphill grade the entire way, but my leg muscles propelled me effortlessly. My breath became slightly more laboured, but not in a way that was worrisome or unpleasant. Instead, I realized that the best way to truly enjoy this body was to push it to its limits.

In much less time than I would have thought possible, I was there, gawking through the chain link at the two jackhammer operators. One of the two was the man I knew to be named Barry. Both were alive and well, working away as if each of them would make it through the day with nothing more than tired muscles and dirty clothes. And, maybe they would.

Now that I'd reached the scene of the envisioned accident, I had to admit to myself that, as sure as I was that Barry was in danger, I had no way of knowing when his accident might occur. Yesterday's precognitive vision occurred just minutes before the actual event, but that didn't mean that today's reenactment had to happen any time soon. It could be days or even weeks from now.

No. The vision I'd experienced had Barry jackhammering about twenty feet further down the bridge from where the two men were working now. From where I stood, I could see that they were using the hammers to break apart the old sidewalk. How long would it take for them to break up twenty feet of concrete? Having never used a jackhammer, I couldn't say, but the only way this vision wouldn't play out today would be if these two men stopped the work they were doing and picked it up again another day. That didn't seem likely. I had to be here today to save Barry's life.

I scanned the area again in search of the cube van, and it was nowhere in sight. Studying my surroundings a bit more, I noticed that there was a coffee shop not very far up the street. I could buy a coffee, sit at one of the shop's outdoor tables, and watch for the arrival of the truck.

I walked in to get the coffee and was suddenly worried because the worksite entrance was not in sight from inside the shop. But the service was quick, and I was outside in no time and, luckily, the table with the best vantage point was unoccupied, so I sat down and studied the situation from behind my coffee cup.

The men with the jackhammers were working about thirty feet down from this end of the bridge. By the time the men reached the point where the incident was to occur, they would be about one-third of the way down the bridge. That meant that I'd have a fair distance to cover once the truck started its fateful roll. I could, of course, try preventing the vehicle from pulling onto the site, or stopping the driver and reminding him to set his emergency brake. But doing so would change the events that I saw in my vision, and I had no idea if I could do that. It would be best if I took action after what I saw in the vision had played out. That meant that I would either have to find a way to be on the worksite or move in very quickly from off-site once the truck started to roll.

At about Eleven O'clock I went back inside the coffee shop and ordered another coffee, as well as soup and a sandwich, and asked the girl behind the counter if she could bring the food out to me when it was ready. When she hesitated, I said "please" and gave her the best smile I could manage. I also tipped her five dollars. She agreed. Pretty sure it was the tip.

By two in the afternoon, I had long finished my second coffee and was starting to feel bad about taking up table space, when the cube van appeared.

CHAPTER EIGHT

When the truck did show up, I didn't recognize it right away. In my vision I saw the truck from the rear. The rear of the truck was a white cube. When it drove past the coffee shop, I saw it from the front, and the cab of the truck happened to be blue. So, I was calmly watching the vehicle as it did a three-point turn and began to back onto the work-site before I realized it was the one I was looking for.

I jumped up and walked briskly toward the site entrance. As I did so, I noticed that the second jackhammer operator was walking toward me. When he reached the gate, he removed his hard hat, set it on a wooden bench just inside the entrance and headed toward two port-a-johns on the other side of the fence, not even looking at me as we passed. Mentally thanking him for providing me with a hat, I picked it up and donned it just as the truck driver jumped down from the cab of his truck. The truck immediately began to roll.

I was going to yell at the driver in the hopes that he could jump back in and stop the truck. I was going to run toward Barry, prepared to physically move him out of harm's way if the driver was unable to act fast enough. I was going to be a hero and save a man's life. And then a hand took hold of my arm.

"What to hell do ya think you're doing, Buddy?" the owner of the hand said.

Glancing over my shoulder at the man, I recognized him as a worker who had pulled the gate open to allow the truck access to the site. I'd seen this happening in a kind of peripheral sense but had paid little attention because my focus had been split between the truck and it's intended victim.

"No, you don't understand…" I started but didn't finish my response. Instead, I wrenched my arm from his grasp and yelled, "Your truck! Stop Your truck" at the driver who was now walking toward us. He turned back and, seeing the truck rolling away, froze in place.

The truck had already picked up speed, its front wheels beginning to turn, causing it to veer toward the unsuspecting worker. The only option now was to run between the truck and the wall of the bridge, hitting Barry with all of my weight and momentum, and hopefully enough force to carry us both from the path of the veering truck. As I picked up speed, I could just make out a shrill voice scream "Barry" over the racket of the jackhammer and then my excitement obscured all sound as I focused on my task.

I moved fast. When I hit Barry, he left the ground and bounced off of me with such force, I had to reach forward and grab him to keep him from being knocked to the ground. His hard hat shot off his head like some kind of projectile. My momentum took me several more steps before I came to a stop, just as I heard the truck slam into the wall behind us. I managed to hold the much lighter Barry in front of me with only the toes of his boots touching the ground. Looking past him, I saw Gary coming toward us, his eyes and mouth gaping.

"Holy Jesus! What the...Jesus Christ!" Gary was babbling as he looked back and forth between Barry and me. I was turning Barry toward me as he had grabbed at his chest with his right hand and I feared he was having a heart attack. With his subsequent gasping intake of breath, I realized that he'd only had the wind knocked out of him.

"You!" Garry exclaimed, recognizing me. "Where the hell did you come from?"

"I, uh…" I managed to say, only now realizing that I might need some explanation for my presence.

"You saved him!" Gary said grabbing both of us, Barry by his left arm and me by my right. Barry was looking back and forth between me and what I assume must have been the truck behind me as he gasped in more breath.

"It happened so fast! He couldn't hear me! How did you…?" Gary said a look of horror still on his face.

"I, uh…" I said.

"What the…" Barry said.

"Barry, are you okay?" Gary asked, turning his attention to his stunned worker.

"Holy Shit, Holy Shit, Holy Shit, Holy Shit!" Barry said, slowly at first but picking up speed with each repetition. He was just starting to realize that someone had saved him from a gruesome fate. "Where did you come from?" Barry asked.

"I, uh…" I began.

"You're that guy Orlie! What the hell?" Gary seemed to be having a little trouble processing everything.

"Holy Shit, Man, thank you!" Barry grabbed me by the shoulders like he was going to pull me into a hug.

"What are you doing here?" Gary asked. I guess he was starting to get things processed.

"I was on Broadway and thought I'd watch the guys work

for a bit. I saw the truck rolling." I was quite pleased that I'd managed to respond with more than "I, uh."

"Thank Christ you did!" Gary said. "I've never seen anyone move that fast!"

I had no response for that other than maybe "I, uh," so I turned and crouched down to look under the truck. The jackhammer had been knocked from Barry's hands when I hit him and was now pinned under the dual rear wheels on this side of the truck. Judging from where the tool lay and where the sidewalk concrete was broken by the jackhammers, Barry would have been crushed between the truck bumper and the bridge wall, or possibly pinned as the jackhammer now was. Either way, it would not have been pretty.

"I better be going," I said.

"Well, come back with your ID. You'll have a job here any time." While he spoke, Gary glanced up at the hard hat I was wearing.

"Thanks. I'll be back," I said.

"Yeah, thanks man! Really! Thanks!" Barry said.

As I exited the worksite, I handed the hard hat to Barry's coworker who was returning from his washroom break and who looked at me with a puzzled expression.

"Uh, thanks," he said.

Walking back to the motel I considered this strange new ability. Getting my head around the idea that I was no longer a ninety-one-year-old man had been hard enough. Now it seemed that I was miraculously reborn with the ability to see into the future. Elsie used to say that everything happened for a reason. I don't know that I ever agreed with her. After all, she usually said it when something crappy had happened. But this was far from crappy. This was incredible!

'I hate to have to admit this my dear, but I'm beginning to think that you may have been right all along,' I said to the memory of my late wife.

'How you could ever have doubted me.' The response was so perfectly Elsie that it was like I could hear her very words in my ears.

I considered the possibility that I was actually dead. I had always been a science fiction and fantasy fan. Maybe this was heaven for someone whose favourite pastime was reading about strange creatures and alien worlds. Perhaps you get to spend your time in the afterlife living an adventure like the ones you've always read about. No, that really didn't make any sense. My five normal senses told me that this was the same city that I had lived in most of my life, although I had to admit that that might not be proof of anything. But, gall-darn-it, I plain just never believed in an afterlife. Despite countless occasions when I pretended to, in order to avoid conflict with our church going society or an argument with a fanatical relative, I just never bought into it. No, when I am indeed dead and gone, there will be nothing afterward. No Heaven, no Hell, and certainly no sci-fi purgatory in a city that looks like Saskatoon, Saskatchewan.

But what was going on? What could possibly have caused these things to happen to me? Why was I reborn and why is it that touching somebody causes me to see their future? For that, I realized, was it. Both visions had occurred as I made physical contact with another person. And in both cases, I saw the future through the eyes of the person with whom I'd come in contact. But for some reason, it didn't happen every time I touched someone. I was pretty sure that the waitress, Demi, had touched me last evening and nothing had flashed before my eyes. So, was it only some people, or only certain types of touches? Hopefully, time would tell.

When Aaron showed up at the motel later that afternoon, I went over to the bar to see if I could get us take-out. I was a little disappointed that Demi wasn't working but happy to find the place entirely cougar-free. I ordered a sandwich with fries for each of us and went next door to the off-sale to pick up a case of beer. Soon I was back in the room and Aaron, and I were eating. Actually, I was eating. Aaron was inhaling.

"Did you find a job?" Aaron asked.

"I talked to the guys at the bridge. They won't hire me without ID."

"You don't have any ID?"

I considered making up a story about losing it or having had it stolen.

"No," I said.

"I know someone who can probably help you," Aaron said.

"Help me?"

"Get you some fake ID," Aaron said.

"I'd need a social insurance number."

"He can probably do that."

"Probably?" I asked

I got that look again. I began to question if what his friend did was legal then thought better of it. Of course, providing someone with fake ID was illegal. Did I really care? I couldn't exactly go into a government office and ask for a new Social Insurance Card. What reason would I give for not having one? If Aaron's friend could get me new identification, that would solve a problem that might otherwise have been insurmountable.

"Thanks!" I said.

"Can I ask you something?" Aaron asked.

"Shoot," I replied.

"Who are you?"

Aaron was looking directly at me, something he wasn't in the habit of doing.

"I told you."

"Well, then, what are you?"

"I don't know what you're asking," I said.

Aaron's next words spewed out of him like they'd been bottled up under pressure and he'd just popped a cork.

"You look like Chris Evans..."

Who?

"...you fight like Captain America…"

Ahhh!

"...you stick up for me, and you don't even know me."

"Well…" I started to respond.

"You talk like it's the first time you've been here, but you walk around town like you know where everything is. You take gobs of money out of the bank, but you say you don't have any ID. You just don't make any sense."

I didn't answer right away. Aaron had looked up from his food when his curiosity had erupted but looked down again once he'd said his piece. The lad had a kind of shyness that didn't seem out of place in a boy of his age. Yet the incongruencies he found in me bothered him enough that he felt compelled to confront me, and confrontation is challenging for most people, let alone someone who is naturally shy. For that reason, I thought I should be truthful with him. Somewhat.

"I guess you could say I'm a guy with a past that I need to put behind me." The truth is almost always the best policy. Just maybe not all of it. "I'm not a bad person Aaron."

I looked over at Aaron and saw a much older person looking back at me through his young eyes.

"And I'm glad you're here" I added. "And I appreciate your help."

Aaron broke eye contact and went back to shovelling food into himself. The popular myth is that kids learn to eat that way because of the competition for food in large families.

"Do you have any brothers or sisters, Aaron?" I asked.

"No. My dad was killed when I was a baby. It's always just been me and mom," Aaron paused, "until that ass-hole showed up."

"He's really that bad?"

"He's a fucking ass-hole!" There was considerable venom in Aaron's voice. "But he makes Mom happy,' he continued in a much quieter voice. "She was lonely for a long time. She deserves to be happy."

"Doesn't she worry about you?"

"Yeah. We text. I let her know I'm okay." Aaron didn't look up. "I told her I have a new friend."

Trying hard not to grin like a big idiot made my face twitch, which made me look like a big idiot.

When we finished eating, we went out for a walk. It was another pleasant evening, and we walked east on 8th street until we reached Boychuk Drive, then crossed the street to head back. As we walked past the Wildwood Golf Course, I asked Aaron if he'd ever golfed. When he replied that he hadn't, I suggested that I'd take him as soon as I had some regular money coming in. I was excited by the prospect of playing golf in this new body. I'd always loved the game and played it as often as I could, but I had to give it up several years back. I figured it was best to quit the game with good memories. By the time I turned eighty, I was losing my ability to smoothly swing a club. I'd watched other guys keep hacking at balls for years after they'd lost the flexibility needed to swing correctly. It wasn't pretty. Continuing to play when your body was telling you to quit was the athletic equivalent of a comb-over. Best to just admit you're bald.

When we got back to the motel, I told Aaron I was going to take a shower and, remembering how long he'd been in the bathroom the night before, I didn't give him the option of going first. Once again, I admired my new self in the mirror. Probably best to not make this a habit. I thought about buying a razor to rid myself of a shadow that was forming on my chin but decided not to worry about it for now. A few whiskers might make me look a little older, and I was totally okay with that. After my shower, I exited the room in a towel, intending to sleep naked as I always had in the past.

"Jesus Christ! Do you have to walk around half naked?" Aaron practically screeched at me. He grabbed his bag and scooted into the washroom slamming the door.

Weird Kid! I thought. *Must've never spent any time in locker rooms.*

When I woke the next morning, Aaron was asleep on top of his covers, fully dressed. I went in to brush my teeth, and when I came out, he was awake.

"Breakfast?"

He nodded and grabbed his bag and went into the washroom.

I once again checked the news on tv, but nothing was mentioned about a highway death.

We walked the same route downtown as we had the day before. Aaron was a quiet kid, who was even quieter in the mornings. I don't think he spoke a single word from the time we got up until we got to the bank on 2nd Avenue and 22nd Street. When he did talk, he didn't waste any words.

"Cash?"

"Maybe later," I replied. I had a feeling I'd best check the newspaper first. We continued on to Midtown Plaza and got breakfast at Starbucks. Once again, I found a paper abandoned on an unoccupied table, and I concluded that the coffee shop made a paper or two available as a service to its customers. I sat and began to scan the news.

My intuition proved to be accurate. A small article on the bottom of page five mentioned an overturned car found in a ditch on highway five. One death. More information to be released by the RCMP pending confirmation of the deceased's identity and notification of next of kin.

I was experiencing a weird mix of emotions. For some reason, my first feeling was of relief. Apparently, I had been anxious about my body being found, and now that it was, I no longer had to worry about it. I was curious. Had I been missed at the condo complex? Had my family been concerned about me? I was sad. Obviously, no one likes to be told of a loved one's passing, even when that loved one was elderly. My family was going to be upset. Oddly, though, my strongest emotion was one of guilt. I couldn't say why, but I felt like I had let them all down by passing away; as if any nonagenarian could put off dying very much longer. But usually, when you die, you're not around afterwards to feel bad about how bad you might be making anyone else feel.

I didn't, however, feel sorry about having taken the money and bank cards off my own corpse. It felt strange to do it at the time, but having had time to think about it, I've since come to the conclusion that I was hurting no one. My offspring were all doing fine and would not miss the small amount that I had accessed with the cards. Aside from that, I felt the money was mine. In the same way that the corpse in that ditch used to be mine and this current body was now mine, my possessions belonged to the consciousness that *is* me, not the body that *was* me. I did, however, decide that I would only attempt to withdraw more money with my cards if Aaron's friend was not able to get me new identification. We went to see him.

We left the Starbucks in Midtown Plaza, walked to the corner of 2nd Avenue and 21st Street, and entered another Starbucks. I was just thinking that a play of my new life would require very few sets, when Aaron stepped in line to place an order.

"I don't need anything," I said.

"Yes, you do," Aaron said. I stepped in line.

When we got to the front of the line Aaron ordered a Venti, Low-Fat, Sugar-Free, Caramel Macchiato with extra caramel, I think. I paid for the concoction. When it was ready, Aaron grabbed the drink and headed to the back of the restaurant where a man sat behind two laptop computers.

He was a thin man with a head of thick black hair. He was wearing a black T-shirt with the likeness of Gabriel Dumont stencilled on the front, and his arms were covered in tattoos. His eyes were flashing back and forth between the two computer screens as he typed on both machines simultaneously, one hand on each.

"Matthew, this is Orville. Orville, Matthew." Aaron reached over the two laptops and set the coffee in front of Matthew.

I held out my hand, and Matthew's right hand flashed up to grab mine. He gave my hand a single shake up and down as his eyes came up to meet mine. The eye contact was extremely brief, lasting only as long as the handshake, but as his eyes returned to his computers, I had the distinct impression that, in that fleeting glance, he had looked deeply into my soul. I had been braced to receive a flash of Matthew's future, but that didn't happen. The feeling of having been so quickly and deeply assessed, however, was almost as unsettling, and I shuddered slightly as a small chill went up my back. Aaron and I sat down across the table from him.

"Aaron tells me you need ID," Matthew said without looking back up from computers. Watching his eyes, it appeared that he was reading both screens as he typed and spoke, all at the same time. Is that even possible?

"Yeah. A social insurance card and a driver's license, I guess," I said.

"Of course," Matthew said. His manner and tone were business-like and polite, but brisk. I got the impression he felt his time was valuable and he was not about to waste it.

"How much and how soon?" I asked. I could be brisk, too.

Matthew's eyes flick up from the screens to look at me briefly. There was the hint of a twinkle in them as he responded.

"Four thousand. Tomorrow."

I was not surprised at the price as I had no idea what the going rate for fake identification was. I was pleasantly surprised, however, at how quickly I would get my new ID.

"Need anything down?" I asked.

"You're with Aaron," Matthew replied, looking at Aaron he said, "Pick it up tomorrow morning."

At that Aaron got up from his seat and headed for the door.

"Thanks," I said as I rose from my chair.

For the first time, Matthew looked at me for more than a split second. There was no expression discernable on his face, but there was something in his eyes that suggested mild disapproval. I had the distinct impression I had been dismissed.

I'd no sooner caught up with Aaron on the street when it occurred to me that I hadn't discussed a new name with Matthew. I didn't want to have new ID with the name Orville on it.

"Wait!" I said. "I didn't give him a new name. And doesn't he need my picture for the driver's license?"

"Matthew will take care of it," Aaron replied. He seemed so confident that everything would be okay that I decided I'd have to just wait and see.

"Let's go for a walk by the river," Aaron said as he continued down the street.

It was another beautiful day.

When Aaron brought me my new identification the next morning, I was surprised to see a photo of the new me on the driver's license. Obviously, Matthew had been able to take my picture without my noticing, I assume with one of his computers, and had doctored it to look like a typical license photo. It showed my address as being on Avenue W, and the date of birth put my age at a little over twenty-seven. Both pieces of ID displayed my new name as Maxwell O Campbell. I liked it.

PART TWO

CHAPTER NINE

I was standing outside the sales office for Saskatoon's newest riverfront development, Meewasin Landing. The office was a temporary structure made of glass, metal and dark, rich looking wood. Behind it, a skeleton of steel reached almost twenty stories into the sky.

I was waiting to shake hands with Henry Bouchard. He was the man and the money behind this aggressive new real estate venture. The man I was waiting with felt it was important that I meet Henry. That seemed reasonable to me, as I had just signed papers making me the owner of the development's penthouse suite.

The salesman, his name was Brad, was very excited. Of course, I knew he would be. I'd learned so when we shook hands upon meeting two hours earlier. When our hands had touched, there was the now-familiar white flash, and I found myself shaking hands with myself. The "me" whose eyes I looked out of in that instant was saying what a great decision the "me" that was looking back had made. Over the past couple of months, I've become quite accustomed to my precognitive flashes, but this was the first time one brought me face-to-face with myself. Of course, the reason for his flash was his excitement at having made the biggest sale of his life.

As far as I've been able to figure out, that's the way these flashes work. Occasionally, when I touch someone, I get a glimpse of the future seen through their eyes. The events I experience are always intensely emotional ones. If nothing of significant emotional importance is going to happen to a person in the near future, as is the case with most people most of the time, I get nothing from him or her but the warm fuzzy feeling that might accompany any friendly handshake. Actually, I still had no idea if there was a limit to how far into the future I could see with these flashes. So far, I had experienced flashes that were no more than a few days from the time of the flashed event. I assumed that there was a time restriction only because I didn't like the possibility that some people might live out the rest of their lives without having an emotionally powerful experience. What would be the point of such a life? I'm beginning to believe, for no particular reason, that the distance into the future I can see is in some way proportional to the intensity of emotion experienced. The stronger the feelings my flash companion experiences, the farther into the future the flash can potentially take place. But this is only speculation at this point. I haven't had enough experience with my gift to be sure of the rules, or for that matter, if there even are any.

The desire to learn more about how these flashes work has turned me into the touchiest person imaginable. I take advantage of any and every opportunity I have to shake hands, hug, or pat somebody on the back. Aside from having the side benefit of making people more accepting of me in general, it seems that casual physical contact is a great way to break barriers and make most people feel recognized and appreciated, touching almost everyone I met resulted in my receiving a good number of these future flashes. Many of them were of intense arguments with loved ones, while others were of passionate encounters with strangers. It seemed that passionate encounters with life partners were seldom intense enough to result in a future flash. Sad.

One flash, in particular, was with a coworker at Walker Construction. True to his word, Gary had given me a job when I returned to the bridge with my new ID. He looked at me a little funny when he saw the name I put on the TD1 form, but when I looked him square in the face and said "Maxwell, Sir," he seemed to accept that the name was uncommon enough to have been the one he had heard two days earlier. He told me I could start the next day, provided I pick up some steel-toed boots and a hard hat and then took me out to meet the guys. I shook hands with all of them as I was introduced and got nothing from them but their names. Well, I got a ridiculously long and enthusiastic handshake from Barry, but that's beside the point. As we were walking back toward the office trailer, we ran into a giant hulk of a man with shaggy blond hair and a massive square jaw. His name was Kyle, and he was dropping off equipment that he'd brought from another site. When Gary introduced him to me his huge hand almost crushed mine, and we flashed.

***

I found myself staring at the long shapely back of a naked woman who was sitting atop a dark-skinned, muscular man who was equally naked. I could feel my heart start to pound in my chest and my vision took on a noticeable scarlet tint.

"Mother Fucker!" I screamed. "I'm going to fucking kill you, you bastard!"

I turned and headed down a hall and in a closet by the back door I found a baseball bat. Grabbing it, I turned back, screaming in rage, and saw the naked figure of the man as he streaked out the front door with a pair of jeans in his hand.

***

And then I was back, pulling my hand from the grip of the smiling giant.

"Oh, sorry buddy! Did I hurt you?" Kyle said, pulling his own hand back like he'd received a shock.

"Oh, no man," I said. "I was just surprised by how big your hand is."

"Yeah, I get that a lot."

Kyle stood at least six and a half feet tall, but even considering his size, his hands seemed unnaturally large. His overwhelming stature, coupled with the shock of seeing his unsettling future, had me so befuddled I could think of nothing else to say but, "How tall are you?"

"A little over six eight," Kyle answered. "You're pretty big yourself."

"Yeah, sure,'" I responded, laughing and feeling like a little boy as I stared up at the grinning brute.

In the course of a brief conversation, I learned that Kyle worked at a Walker Construction site on the University Campus and that he was very excited about playing rugby. I was just trying to imagine why anyone would ever play rugby against a guy his size, when I found myself agreeing to show up at a practice for the team that evening. I said goodbye to the two men, and as I walked away, I asked myself why, with all the unbelievable things that were happening to me, I thought it was a good time to join a rugby team. I answered myself that it might be the only way I could keep that friendly giant from beating another man to a pulp with a baseball bat.

When I got to the pitch that evening, I found Kyle towering over a group of guys, leading them in some kind of chant. I learned pretty quickly that it was a drinking song and that rugby practices were as much about drinking beer as they were about playing rugby. Kyle introduced me around, and I shook hands with my new acquaintances. Thankfully, not one of them gave me a future flash. I couldn't handle dealing with anyone else's future when I already had Kyle to worry about.

I had never been a big sports fanatic in my earlier life, and rugby was definitely a sport I'd paid little attention to. Frankly, what I knew of it made me think it was a rather silly game. It seemed to me that it was played by a bunch of rugged thugs wearing shorts and T-shirts whose only reason for showing up was to make football players look like a bunch of pansies. I was sure that the rules of the game were very simple; essentially, one man takes possession of the ball and then the players from both teams beat him to death. Then another man gets the ball and he, in turn, is brutally assassinated. Occasionally, a man might get the ball and somehow avoid being murdered. He will run around a bit and then kick the ball, after which all the players on his team will jump up and down and cheer. Following that, the players from both sides take a moment to drag their dead off the field.

When I admitted my ignorance of the game to the guys, one member of the group was chosen to take me aside and give me the basics. This enthusiastic fellow's name was Lucas, and he was from Australia. He proceeded, in a very animated way, to talk at a rate that I would not have been able to follow even without his thick accent. He went on excitedly for quite some time, not giving me a chance to interject. I honestly didn't understand a single word until he ended with a few words I did manage to catch.

"Let's play rugby, Mate!" he exclaimed, slapping me on the shoulder and turning to run back out on the field.

I followed him out and was greeted by grinning faces all around.

"So, you know how to play rugby?" one of the guys asked.

The wide-eyed look of panic on my face made them all break into fits of laughter as they slapped my back and punched me in the arm. Laughing loudly, Kyle threw his arm around Lucas' shoulder and dragged him away while mussing the Australian's hair with one of his massive hands.

A short, thick man named Rick grabbed my arm and

proceeded to explain what was going to happen in the next play and what I was expected to do. Before long, I was having the most fun I'd had in about fifty years, as I ran, tackled, shouted, and laughed my way to more bruises than I'd ever had in my life.

And then, after a play that found almost every player in a pile in the middle of the field, everyone got up except one giant hulk of a man. Kyle was lying face down in the grass with one arm shielding his face and the other reaching back and holding his right hip.

"Oh shit, it's his back again," one of the men said.

Lucas knelt down next to Kyle and asked clearly, "You okay, Mate?"

"Yeah, give me a minute," Kyles huge voice rumbled out from under his arm. He slowly got up on his knees, and Lucas and another guy helped him to his feet. "I'm sorry guys, but that's it for me tonight."

Everyone groaned, and several reached out to pat him on the back.

"I should be going too, guys," I said. "I'm starting a new job tomorrow, and I should try to get a good night's sleep. Besides, I think I'll drive this big bastard home and make sure he's okay."

"Awe, I'm okay," Kyle said, but he followed that with a grunt that said he really wasn't.

"It's okay, man," I said. "I'll drive you home in your car and then walk home from there. You don't look like you should be driving." I grabbed his arm, put it over my shoulder and began guiding him toward the parking lot.

Kyle didn't argue and based on the set of his huge jaw as he limped along, he was worse off than he was letting on. It was pretty obvious, however, that this was something he'd experienced before. He wasn't the first large man I'd known who'd had back issues. There was a price to be paid for carrying around that much weight every day of your life.

Driving his vehicle home wasn't really going to do anything to help ease the pain he was experiencing. Of course, the real reason I wanted to take him home was that I was pretty sure his wife or girlfriend was going to be surprised to find him showing up before the practice was supposed to be over.

Kyle's vehicle was a Dodge 1500 pick-up truck, and he had a tough time squeezing his huge body into the passenger side. By the time he was in, his forehead was beaded with sweat and he looked exhausted. He was in a lot of pain. When I got in on the driver's side, I found the seat jammed as far back and down as it would go and I searched for the switch that would bring my feet within comfortable range of the pedals.

When we pulled up in front of Kyle's house on the south end of Lansdowne Avenue, the sky was beginning to darken. I helped Kyle out of the truck and handing him his keys, I said goodnight, knowing that he would soon encounter something that would make him completely forget about his sore back.

I walked North slowly and glanced back several times until I saw Kyle enter his house. As soon as he was inside, I jogged back and waited to one side of the walk at the bottom of the steps leading into the house. I no sooner got there when I heard a bellowing like an angry bull coming from inside and before I knew it a naked man came flying out, launching himself off the front step like he hoped to take flight, and landing in the middle of the front lawn in a full-out run. I stepped onto the walkway in front of the door, and before I could prepare myself, I was hit by a bus.

Ok. So, I know it was Kyle that ran over me as he bounded out of the house, but, honest to God, it felt like I'd been hit by a very large, very fast-moving vehicle. We tumbled head over heels a couple of times and came to rest with me laying on top of Kyle. He was groaning and screaming at the same time, and he lifted me off of himself like I was made of bubble wrap.

"Max? What the fuck?" the bus said.

"Stop, Kyle, you can't hurt him," I said.

Kyle picked up the bat he had dropped when he ran over

me and bounded to the sidewalk in search of the naked man. He was already at the end of the block and didn't look like he planned on stopping to put his pants on any time soon.

"Fuuuuuck!" Kyle bellowed and threw the bat side-arm in the direction of the running man, but his aim was a little high. I don't know where that bat came down, I just hope nobody got hurt.

The rest of the evening was full of yelling, screaming and crying by both Kyle and his wife. As the evening progressed, I learned that Kyle's wife's name was Fucking Bitch and his pet names for her were a bunch of words I don't feel comfortable repeating. I stayed long enough to watch her gather up most of her clothes from the lawn where Kyle had thrown them and get into the car when her mother came to pick her up. I then sat with a huge crying man and drank half of a big bottle of whisky. I made sure my half was smaller. Later, as I opened the door to leave, Kyle was lying face down on the couch, sobbing quietly.

I felt like a badly bruised piece of crap the next morning as I started my first job in twenty-six years. As it turned out, I never ended up working on the bridge. By the time I got to work the next morning, word of Kyle's problems had arrived ahead of me. I learned that the naked man was one of Kyle's coworkers on the university site. It was decided before I arrived that I would be going to work in his place and the naked man would be coming to work on the bridge. The naked man was very fortunate. People kept saving his life.

When I met the new crew on campus, I got my first future flash of a sexual nature. There was something distinctly unsettling about meeting a person for the first time and instantly having knowledge of them that was so deeply personal.

The next significant flash occurred about a week later. I had rented a two-bedroom apartment on 9th Street near Broadway and offered the extra room to Aaron. Not only could I not bear to let the little guy go back to his life on the street, but I'd also quickly grown accustomed to his company. I liked having him around. When I showed Aaron the suite and opened the door to his room, he looked as though he was going to cry. Up to that point, he had thought I was just showing off my new accommodations. He threw his arms around me, trapping my arms at my side and gave me a tremendous squeeze.

Oddly, contact with Aaron did cause me to experience the white flash that normally precedes a vision, however, I found myself in the bedroom with the little guy and still fully in possession of my faculties. It seemed that when the moment of emotional excitement was happening at the same time I was in physical contact with someone, the contact triggered the white flash but not a shared vision. However, that was not the *significant* flash that I had referred to. That one happened shortly after Aaron and I had moved in.

We were sleeping on the floors of our rooms those first few nights, as I hadn't had time to purchase furniture. I was returning home from a trip to the grocery store when I encountered a fellow tenant at the front door. She was an elderly woman whom I knew to live on the second floor of the building and she too, had just been out shopping. I'd offered to carry her bag up to her suite and as I set it down just inside her door, she grabbed me by the wrist and gave it a grateful little squeeze. That was when the significant flash occurred.

***

I was sitting at a table with a pen in my hand. In front of me was an iPad showing the winning number from Wednesday's Lotto 649. A ticket next to the computer had four numbers circled on it, and I was drawing a circle around the fifth. My white and age-spotted hand flew to the iPad and slid the page on it up to show the amount for five matched numbers, $6,800.80. Two lines up on the table of winning numbers the page showed 6 of 6, 1 - SK, $40,497,949.90. I looked again at the winning numbers and...

***

I was back, smiling down at this beautiful old lady who was praising me for being such a helpful young man.

"I'm sorry to interrupt, ma'am, but do you have a pen and paper?" I blurted out.

"Why yes, right on the wall by your shoulder," the lady replied.

I quickly grabbed the pen, which dangled on a string from a notepad on the wall, and scribbled down the winning numbers, being careful to hide what I was writing with my left hand.

Tearing the note off the pad, I thanked the lady and, grabbing my bag, quickly ran up the stairs to my suite. I was so excited all I could bring myself to do was pace rapidly back and forth from my empty dining room to my equally empty living room.

'Am I wrong to do this, Elsie?' I asked the presence in my mind that used to cause me sadness. I still thought of Elsie all the time, but where I used to think only of how lonely I was and how much I missed her, I now found myself sharing with her the wonders of this new life and the people in it. I imagined hearing her tell me, the way she did when she was still alive, that everything happens for a reason.

'But I feel like I'm cheating!' I thought back at her.

'Don't be foolish, you silly man!' I heard her voice like she was standing next to me. *'Do you think being reborn in a new, younger body isn't cheating? Go buy a blessed ticket!'*

I went and bought a ticket.

So here I was, the most fortunate man alive and the new owner of a piece of real estate I never would have dreamed of in my former life. And, God help me, I was finding myself irritated at being made to wait. Before long, the man I waited for ended his call.

"Mr. Bouchard," Salesman Brad said as he bounded toward the other man. Brad was starting to remind me of the Bugs Bunny cartoon where the little dog jumps around in front of the larger dog. "This is Max Campbell. Max is the new owner of the Meewasin Landing Penthouse, Sir. Max, this is Henry Bouchard."

Brad used the French pronunciation of 'Henry.' I hoped I'd never have to use the man's first name. I was terrible at accents.

"Mr. Campbell," Bouchard said as he extended his hand.

The flash I experienced while shaking his hand shook my world.

CHAPTER TEN

I was in a dimly lit room surrounded by naked people. They were gathered in groups of twos and threes and were groping and grinding against one another. There was a pounding, like the sound of muffled bass from music in a distant room. The room was warm, I was covered in sweat, and I was smiling. No. I was leering.

As I looked to my right, I locked eyes with another man. He was engaged with another young woman, but the look in his eyes appeared to be one of confusion and perhaps intoxication rather than lust.

My gaze dropped to the small figure before me. It was a girl who looked to be a teenager, and she was as naked as everyone else in the room. Tears were running down her cheeks in muddy rivers from her overly made up eyes. I never, ever want to have to describe to anyone what this young person was doing to me.

As is always the case, my heart was pounding. The pure lascivious joy I was experiencing was overwhelming and...

***

I was back in the present, and as I wrenched my hand from Bouchard's, I turned my head and vomited on the sidewalk next to the man. As I continued to turn away from him, I doubled over and heaved again. Very little came out with the second effort, but I still felt it hadn't expelled all the sickness from me. As I straightened and turned back to the man, I gasped for air past a heart that had risen and become lodged in my throat.

I looked at Bouchard, who was looking back at me with an expression of surprise and horror. It didn't compare, however, to the horror with which I viewed him.

"Are you okay, Max?" Brad was asking.

"Mr. Campbell?" Bouchard queried.

I couldn't respond. It felt like someone the size of Kyle was standing on my chest, and I could not catch my wind. I continued to stare at Bouchard with a look of revulsion I didn't bother to hide. In all my years I'd known many people I feared were evil. This was the first time I knew with absolute certainty that I was in the presence of a devil.

"Max, What's wrong?" Brad asked.

"Nothing, nothing, I'm okay," I finally managed to get out. I was locked in a staring contest with Bouchard who now seemed to be looking back with a mild expression of curiosity. "I'm sorry, I have to go."

I turned to head to where my new truck was parked. I had only taken a few steps when I found I could go no further. I could not stop myself from doing what I did next any more than I could ever forget the disgusting scene of that future flash.

Wheeling back around I threw myself at Bouchard and

79

grabbing him by the front of his jacket and pulling his face toward mine I screamed at him.

"I know what kind of sick, disgusting bastard you are, Bouchard! If I ever see you around a young girl, any young girl, I'll, I'll…"

"What Mr. Campbell? What will you do?" His look was now one of incredulity. "And what is it you think you know, Mr. Campbell?"

But again, I was speechless. All I could do was glare at him with a look of hatred that should have scorched his face.

"Interesting," Bouchard said. "Very interesting."

I pushed him away from me with a force that would have knocked a smaller man on his backside. I stalked away from him and past the bewildered salesman who managed only to express a couple of breathy, questioning "Wha?" sounds.

To this point, the fact that I was able to share the feelings that my flash subjects experienced was something of a fascinating curiosity to me. Feeling the rage of a man who has caught his wife cheating is disturbing, but not unexpected. Experiencing the elation of an old woman as she discovers her winning lottery numbers is just plain fun. Sharing the excitement of someone enjoying the company of a willing and probably equally excited partner could be embarrassing, but it was only that. But this feeling of erotic joy over an experience with a young and frightened child brought me nothing but powerful feelings of revulsion. I kept shuddering as if I was cold and the sense of something crawling on my skin had me fighting the urge to scratch at myself. Twenty minutes of vigorous scrubbing in the shower, when I got home, didn't make me feel much better.

At work the next morning I found myself distracted. I know. I'd won a lottery and I was still working, so you think I must be crazy. If I am crazy, and I'm not about to argue it, that's probably not the best proof one could come up with. I do claim to have died and come back to life in a new and improved body, after all. Oh, and I can see people's future by touching them. But, you see, the guys I worked with at Walker Construction and, to a greater extent, the men on my rugby team were now a huge part of my life. Because of these new friendships I felt connected to the world in a way I hadn't felt in years, and I was reluctant to give them up. So, despite having to tell two or three people a day to bugger off because I wasn't going to lend, or give, them any money, I had continued to show up for work every day and attend every rugby game and practice. Besides that, I found working on a construction site to be a new and rewarding experience in its own right. I was enjoying every minute of it.

But on this day, I was too distracted to really put my heart into my work. I couldn't get the flash from the previous day out of my mind. The look of horror in the young girl's eyes haunted me. The knowledge that accosting Bouchard the way I did had done nothing to change her fate disturbed me even more. I was pretty sure I was unable to change the events of a flash, which meant that even if I found a way to intervene in Bouchard's little party, I could only affect change after the events of the vision I had experienced. That meant that nothing I did could keep the girl from living that horror. But I did have a strong urge to test my theory by killing Bouchard.

And what about the other people involved? There were other young women, unwilling participants also, I felt reasonably certain. And there were other men. Bouchard was a sick bastard with some equally sick friends.

'What do I do, Elsie?'

I tried to imagine what her response would be.

'Everything happens for a reason, Orville. You have to do something to help those girls. It must be why you are here, and why you know what you know.'

I had to do something. I obviously couldn't go to the police with what I knew. How would I say I came by this knowledge?

"Well, you see, I died and was reborn in a younger body,

and now I can see the future." And the future is filled with straitjackets, locked doors, and lots of psychotherapy. No. Whatever I decided to do, I would have to do alone.

I knew only one person involved, so I'd have to start by finding out all I could about him. Bouchard was a prominent businessman in Saskatoon, and the newspapers were bound to have articles about him. I doubted any article would mention his interest in abusing young girls, but they might refer to other men that he associates with, men that might share his sick proclivities. But something told me this method of investigation would be too slow. Every day spent in research might be another day of hell for those girls.

Who could possibly know what I needed to know other than Bouchard himself? Do people that do such things allow knowledge of their activities to leek to the public? Obviously not, or the problem would have solved itself and Bouchard would be in prison. But guys like that couldn't just grab a few girls off the street and invite them to party. They must have a network of conspirators that help them find girls that fit their needs. They must be part of an underworld that...

Holy cow, Orville! I hadn't yet begun thinking of myself as Max. *You already know the guy to talk to about this!*

I could hardly wait for the day to end so I could talk to Aaron. For the first time, I questioned why I hadn't quit my job as soon as I'd won the lottery. As I left at the end of the day, I told the foreman I might not be back.

The next morning, Aaron and I went to see Matthew. We found him sitting in the same chair, in the same Starbucks, where I had first met him.

"Orville."

It was odd that he didn't use my new name, since he was the one who gave it to me.

"Matthew"

Once again, our handshake was one quick up and down

jerk as the man behind the computers glanced briefly at my soul.

"What can I do for you today?"

"I'd like to ask you a few questions, if I may." It never hurts to be polite.

"Ask." I was beginning to understand why Matthew and Aaron got along. Neither was inclined to waste words.

"I'm wondering if you know anything about a man named Henry Bouchard," I said.

"I know he wouldn't be happy with the way you pronounce Henry." Matthew pronounced it properly. "Why do you think I would know anything about that ass-hole?"

"Well, you know he's an arse-hole."

"Arse-hole?" Matthew's laugh was a single bark. "Do you even live in this world?"

Just visiting, I think.

"I've heard some shit about him," Matthew said.

"What kind of shit?" Yeah. I said it.

Matthew glanced up at my soul again. What was it about this guy that made me think he knew more about me than I did?

"Why do you want to know?" Matthew asked.

"I have reason to believe he might be hurting people."

Matthew glanced at Aaron, and I had the impression that they had an instantaneous telepathic conversation about me. Matthew wrote on a post-it note and handed it to me.

"Go and talk to Daniel at this address. I believe you will find that he feels the way you do about Bouchard. I will instruct him to share what he knows with you. Aaron, stay. I need you."

I turned to leave and then turned back.

"What's this going to cost me?" I asked.

"For now, let's call it a favour," Matthew answered without

looking up.

I had been dismissed.

The house on Avenue E was a beautiful century-old two-story. The exterior had been recently upgraded, judging by the vinyl siding and new metal soffit, fascia and gutters. It appeared that what was originally attic had been converted to living space, as a new window had been added in the gable facing the street. The yard was tidy and spartan and the grass well-manicured. The house looked warm and inviting, except for a six-foot high chain link fence that framed the lot. The gate at the front of the property sported a latch of a sort I'd never seen before, but before I had time to trouble over how it might be unbolted, the front door opened, and an entirely uninviting individual appeared.

Judging by the door frame, he was well over six feet tall and very lean. He wore dark baggy blue jeans that looked several sizes too big and a black hooded sweatshirt from which the sleeves had been removed. He must have spent a good deal of money having both of his arms covered in tattoos, and he wanted his investment out where it could be enjoyed. The front of the sweatshirt displayed a design I had never seen before. He stepped forward to the front of the porch and leaned against a pillar, crossing his arms. He stared at me with a look of utter contempt and said nothing.

"I'm here to see Daniel," I said.

Still nothing.

"Matthew sent me," I said.

The tall, dark man straightened from his slouch and at the same time, the latch on the gate clicked loudly. He didn't move in my direction, so I swung the gate open and strode toward him, trying to look more confident than I felt. As I approached him, I could see that his neck was also tattooed. The tattoo was a smaller version of the design on his sweatshirt and was just large enough to cover his Adam's apple. He stared directly into my eyes as I approached him and just before I reached him he turned and stepped back into the house. This pleased me because I wasn't sure if we were going to shake hands or if he was going to pull out a knife and stab me. I followed him into the house.

The inside of the house was also more welcoming than my new friend. Like the outside, the interior had undergone a recent renovation. The paint was fresh, and the heavy oak door frames and hardwood floors had been refinished. To my left, a double-wide doorway opened into what seemed to be a living room from which I could hear voices and music. Straight ahead was a short hallway that appeared to lead to a kitchen area. Above the entrance to this hallway hung a black flag with the same graphic that was displayed on my friend's sweatshirt and neck. To my right, a set of stairs led to the second floor. My friend looked at me and moved his head with a barely perceptible jerk, just enough to indicate I was to go up. Despite looking to be twenty pounds lighter than me, this man was incredibly intimidating. I was able to determine this by the degree to which I felt intimidated. I was very much relieved when he didn't follow me up.

At the top of the stairs, I found a short hallway with a closed door on each side. The hall opened at the other end into a large room. I stepped in.

The room's walls were covered with a stunning assortment of First Nations art and various other hangings. These adornments were a perfect complement to the heavy oak and hardwoods. On the wall directly opposite the entrance was another flag with that unique graphic. In contrast to much of the decor, one end of the room was full of fitness equipment, including a treadmill and what appeared to be a cross-country ski simulator, a universal gym and several weights. On the other side of the room was a large oak desk, some chairs and a couch. A man was getting up from behind the desk.

The fitness equipment was definitely not just decoration. The man was, in fact, almost exactly the same size as me, a couple of inches over six feet tall and very well muscled, however, his somewhat darker skin than mine made his muscles look harder and more formidable. He had the same Adam's apple tattoo on his neck as the friendly guy at the door, but his arms were bare. He approached me in a very business-like manner, extending his hand to shake.

"Max, very nice to meet you!" he said, grasping my hand firmly and giving it one quick shake. My shock when looking at his face must have been obvious because he followed up with, "Yes, we're twins."

"Uh, Daniel. Yes. Nice to meet you, too," I said. My shock was only, in part, surprise at seeing the face of Matthew looking back at me. It was due, also, to the professional friendliness with which I'd been greeted, not at all what I expected after the reception at the front door.

"Matthew tells me you're interested in what I can tell you about Henry Bouchard."

"Yes, I am, but if you don't mind my asking, what are…?" I paused, not knowing how to phrase my question, so I glanced at the tattoo on his neck and then gestured to the flag on the wall behind him.

"Oh? That?" Daniel responded, immediately understanding what I was trying to ask. "We are Rebellion. We're an organization dedicated to the protection and direction of First Nations and Metis youth in Saskatoon." He said it like it was a catch-phrase, something he'd said many times before.

"Oh, I've heard of The Rebellion," I said, trying to keep my friendly smile from twitching as I said it. What I knew of the Rebellion from things I'd heard in my former life was that they were a gang of ruffians that terrorized residents on the city's west side.

"Not 'The Rebellion'," Daniel said, with a slight sharpness to his voice. "Just 'Rebellion'. And don't believe everything you've heard about us. We work to keep our young people out of the hands of the other gangs and to provide them better things to devote their efforts toward."

Every criminal thinks he's justified in his actions, I thought as I tried hard to keep my skepticism from showing on my face.

"Sorry. Rebellion," I said, dropping the 'The.' "So, what can you tell me about Bouchard?"

"I can tell you he's an absolute bastard!" Daniel exclaimed.

So much for controlling my facial expressions. My shock at the venom in Daniel's description had to have been obvious.

"Why do you say that?" I asked, trying to get our conversation back to the professional tone with which it had started.

"Before I say more, let me ask why you're interested in him," Daniel said, once again adopting his business-like manner.

"I had the pleasure of meeting him the other day and got the feeling he wasn't a very nice person," I said. When Daniel said nothing in response, I added, "I got the impression he might be up to no good."

Daniel laughed in obvious amusement. I was noticing that people often seemed to find me amusing.

"I think I see why Matthew likes you," he said.

"Likes me?" I asked, incredulously.

"Oh, he likes you. You would know if Matthew didn't like you."

Actually, I would have thought Matthew didn't like me. I didn't bother saying so.

"So, what can you tell me?" I prodded.

"Well, other than being a big-shot-ass-hole-white-man, we have reason to believe he's got something to do with some young girls that have gone missing in recent months. Some of our guys have seen his Quebecois thugs creeping around our neighbourhood. We've tried questioning them, but they're pretty tough. And they're armed."

I felt a chill crawl up my back. The girls in my flash with Bouchard could very well have been First Nation or Metis.

"Have you talked to the police?"

"Shit, aren't you naive? Do we look like we spend a lot of time consulting with the police? No one cares about our missing girls but us. Their families go to the police, and some papers get filled out, and then the police go back to their doughnuts." It was obvious that the subject was one that Daniel felt very strongly about, but aside from raising his voice slightly, he retained his professional demeanour. After pausing to collect his thoughts, he continued. "Actually, there is one cop who's been looking into things, but he's the only one, and I don't think he's getting very far."

"Do you know his name?" I asked.

"Tkatchuk. He's young. He's not very experienced. He's the best the police can assign to searching for our girls." His voice was edged with sarcasm.

"Is there anything else you can tell me about Bouchard?"

"We know that aside from real estate he's involved in a few other businesses. He's part owner in Wonderwall. It's a nightclub on 24th Avenue. We've tried getting in there, unsuccessfully." He paused and looked at me thoughtfully. "There are places a good-looking white boy might be able to go that we can't."

He looked me straight in the eyes at that point like he was searching for something there. He had a little bit of his brother's ability to look past a person's outer self. I tried not to shiver noticeably.

"Are you sure you want to get involved with this guy. You might look like a Hollywood superhero, but you really don't seem like you know what you're doing here. No offence intended."

"Well, I guess I really don't know what I'm doing here, but if he's got something to do with these missing girls, somebody needs to do something. And you're right. There are probably places I can go that you can't."

Daniel reached out and put his hand on my shoulder. No

forward-flash accompanied the contact.

"Here's my card," Daniel continued. "It has my cell number on it. Call me if you learn anything and, if you give me your number, I'll do the same." He looked at me expectantly.

"Oh! Sorry! I don't have a phone," I said.

"What? Who doesn't have a phone?" Daniel laughed again. "Get yourself a phone, man! Join the twenty-first century!"

The hand on my shoulder gently turned me toward the short hallway.

My friend from the front door was waiting on the small landing halfway down the stairs. I smiled at him as I moved past and his face darkened, his glare growing more intense. It felt like the beginning of a healthy new relationship. Shivers walked up and down my spine like little feet and didn't stop until the gate at the end of the walk closed behind me.

Once back in my truck, I thought about going to the young cop, Tkatchuk. But what would I tell him? What reason would I give for sticking my nose into his investigations? Matthew and Daniel seemed willing to answer my questions about a matter that should, for all intents and purposes, have been no concern of mine. But a cop is bound to ask me questions I just wasn't prepared to answer. I decided I'd head home and talk to Aaron about what I'd learned.

On the way home, I stopped and bought a brand-new cell phone.

"I can't believe you got a phone," Aaron said.

"I got tired of being told to join the twenty-first century. I'm going to need your help learning how to work this thing."

"It's an iPhone. All you do is tap the icons."

I flipped the phone over in my hands and pondered its function. There were buttons on the slimmer sides, and one larger round one on what I figured was the front. The young lady at the phone store had quickly reviewed how everything worked, but she did it as if I already knew what she was showing me, and it made no sense to me whatsoever. Aside from that, I was a little flustered at the time, partially because she was flirting with me, but also because she kept laughing at me. Did I mention I'm growing tired of people laughing at me?

I pressed the larger round button and the screen lit up brightly. On it were several small square images that I assumed were the icons. I tapped one of them, and the screen suddenly showed a map. I growled a bit in frustration and Aaron came over and took the phone from me. He then began to patiently train me in the wonders of modern communication.

After what seemed like several hours, but was probably much less, I felt I had a grasp on the basic workings of the phone. Aaron was a patient teacher, and he had the advantage of knowing that I really did know absolutely nothing about these tools. He also knew how I felt about being laughed at, so he managed to get through the lesson with only a couple of quiet chuckles.

I grabbed a beer from the fridge and moved into the living room, taking a seat on the couch. Aaron followed with a Diet Coke and took his regular place in a big armchair, legs tucked up underneath him. Even in my new body, my legs would be asleep in about two minutes sitting like that.

"What did you learn from Daniel?" Aaron asked.

"Learned he doesn't like Bouchard any more than Matthew does. They're twins."

"Yeah, crazy, eh?" Aaron responded. "I guess you couldn't tell them apart before the accident."

"Accident?"

"The one that crippled Matthew. Don't tell me you never noticed his wheelchair!"

I must have looked a bit sheepish.

"How do you think you're going to be some kind of investigator dude with this Bouchard thing when you don't even notice when someone's in a wheelchair?" Aaron laughed.

"Oh, for crying out loud! Why in tarnation is everything about me so gall-darn funny?" I shouted.

"I've told you! It's this 'gall-dern' and 'tarnation' stuff mostly. It's not a bad thing, but you sound like you just climbed down out of the Ozarks. You can't blame people for noticing. It's weird."

"You can't tell me I'd seem more sophisticated if every second word I said was 'Fuck', like everybody else these days!"

"Holy fuck! Orville said 'fuck'!" Aaron practically squealed with delight. This was a side of Aaron I'd never seen before.

I made a quick move as if to get off the couch, and Aaron shot out of his chair and down the hall toward his room. I sat there and fumed a bit. After a minute or so Aaron poked his head out from the hallway to see if it was safe to come out.

"It's safe, you little twit," I said.

Aaron returned to his chair.

"Sorry, Max. It really is just that you talk differently than most people. I'm sure everyone just thinks it's cute." Aaron had adopted my new name fully as soon as I'd received my new ID from Matthew. He said it suited me. I guess "Orville" will be reserved for teasing purposes only.

"Yeah. From now on when Matthew or Daniel laugh at me, I'll try to remember they just think I'm cute."

Aaron laughed. With me, this time, not at me.

"What do you know about Matthew's accident?"

"The story goes that Matthew and Daniel stole a car when they were teenagers and drove it into a telephone pole. Matthew went to the hospital, and Daniel went to jail. He was driving. Daniel, I mean."

We sat in silence a bit. I realized that I didn't have a clue what Matthew's and Daniel's lives might have been like. Mine had been the typical life of the white Canadian man of the twentieth century, with none of the challenges that faced the average aboriginal man of my age. Of any age, for that matter.

And, for the most part, I lived my life oblivious of their world, I'm embarrassed to admit.

"I wonder if they would have been more alike now if Matthew wasn't crippled," Aaron said.

"They are so different it's bizarre to see them each wearing the same face," I said.

"So, what about Bouchard?" Aaron prompted.

"Daniel believes he's involved in the disappearance of some Metis girls. I think he probably is."

"Tell me again why you think Bouchard is Saskatoon's biggest bad-ass?'

I tried to give Aaron the same withering look he so often gave me. I hadn't told him why I dislike Bouchard. As close as the two of us were becoming, I still hadn't shared any of my unusual secrets with the boy. Not so much because I didn't trust him, but because I knew he found me strange as it was. I didn't want him to think I was crazy.

"He owns a nightclub named Wonderwall. I'm going to have to go and check it out. See if anything going on there seems unusual. Daniel says he's heard rumours about the place, but he and his people aren't welcome there."

"No kidding. Their tattoos don't help them any."

"Maybe they could wear turtleneck sweaters. At least hide the tattoos on their Adam's apples."

"Oh my God! You are so…" Aaron began, but catching my expression, cut off what he was going to say in time to save his life. He was quiet for a moment and then said, "I think I know someone who can check the place out better than you can."

"OK, Mr. Resourceful. Get your spy on the job," I said.

Aaron got up and went to his room, returning in a moment with his backpack. I couldn't help but notice as he left, that he had a slightly worried look on his little face. That made me a little bit worried, too. My worry got a bit worse when he didn't come back that night.

CHAPTER ELEVEN

It wasn't the first time Aaron had spent the night somewhere other than our apartment, so I told myself, after noting his absence the next morning, that there was nothing to worry about. In the past when Aaron had spent the night elsewhere, I fought the urge to act fatherly and reprimand or question him. After all, before we met, Aaron had been living on the street. I could not even have done the "At least give me a call and let me know where you are" thing, because until the day before, I'd had no phone. Now I wished I had at least asked him to keep in touch. I took out my phone and fumbled my way to sending him a text message that said, "Everything good?" I then tried to put any worry out of my mind as I waited for a reply.

I sat on the balcony with a cup of coffee and enjoyed the

pleasant chirping of sparrows in the trees. This morning it seemed the trees held more birds than leaves. I thought again about going and talking to the cop, Tkatchuk. Could anyone just go and ask a police officer about his investigations? It wasn't as if I was a private detective. If I was a private detective, could I then go and ask a cop about his investigations? I really had no idea. I suspected that most real private detectives did little more than take pictures of cheating spouses. Everything I knew about police or private eye investigations I'd learned from TV and movies. Should I go to Bouchard and once again challenge him? What would that get me? All of this was so unlike my original life that I felt completely out of my element. I had spent almost forty years running a printing press. What did I know about investigating missing girls? I was feeling a mild queasiness in my stomach. And then it hit me! I was afraid!

I knew by the time I was Seventy or so that I had missed a lot of life's opportunities because I'd let a little fear get in the way. Twenty years ago, the thought of what I'd missed actually bothered me very little. After all, my life was pretty good. What did I have to complain about? But, now, I'd been given a second chance at life, in a new and much-improved body, and with a little added precognition thrown in to boot. What right did I have to let a little fear hold me back from doing what had to be done? If Elsie was right all along, and everything does happen for a reason, then the most likely reason I was here was to save this city's young women from a creep like Henry Bouchard. I pictured my late wife's face with a big smile on it as I gulped the rest of my coffee and strode from my apartment.

I swung past my future penthouse home and got the address of Bouchard's office from the huge sign posted out front. His office building, recently built from the look of it, was located on 103rd Street in Sutherland, just west of the Muskeg Lake Urban Reserve. I know that's not it's official name, but

I'll be darned if I can remember what its real name is, and I probably couldn't pronounce it if I did.

I parked on the street in front of the building, even though there was parking available in the lot beside the building. It was a Friday morning, so I figured somebody would be in the office, but when I entered, I found the only desk in the small reception room unoccupied. Looking around I noticed a tiny camera in one corner that was pointed directly where I stood in front of the desk. As I complimented myself on my improved powers of observation, a pretty, young woman entered the room from a door behind the desk. The door swung shut behind her.

"Can I help you?" She had a slight, but noticeable French accent, which seemed to render her unable to pronounce H's.

"I'd like to speak with Henry Bouchard," If the young lady hadn't had a French accent, I might have tried to pronounce his name correctly.

"Do you have an appointment?"

The way she said 'appointment' was really cute.

"No."

"I'm sorry, but Monsieur Bouchard is not here right now. Would you like to make an appointment?" Okay, everything she said was really cute.

Focus, Orville!

"Can you tell me where I might find him?"

"Hmmm. Could you wait for one minute, please?" She got up and exited through the back door and before the door closed, I noticed what looked like a hallway. I scanned the room, trying to take note of as much as possible while I waited. I didn't really think that the number of pictures on the wall or the filing cabinet in the corner was significant, but I figured that being a bit more observant was a good habit for me to cultivate.

The door opened, and the young lady stepped back into the room.

"I'm sorry, but no one knows where Monsieur Bouchard is this morning. You could leave a message or make an appointment."

I considered sticking around to see how many times I could get her to say "appointment" but instead said, "I'll make an appointment." The young lady sat down at her computer.

"Monsieur Bouchard is not available until Wednesday afternoon. Is that good with you?"

"Fine," I said, even though I didn't actually feel it was fine. "My name is Max Campbell. I just bought the penthouse suite at The Meewasin."

"Good, Monsieur Campbell. Monsieur Bouchard will see you Wednesday afternoon at 1:30. Fine?" Did she seem a little nervous?

"Fine," I said as I turned to leave.

The entire experience seemed a little strange. I'd swear the pretty, young receptionist was typing my name even before I had given it to her. Also, these days everyone has a cell phone with them every minute of the day. How is it then that Bouchard's people could be out of contact with him during a business day?

Despite my improved powers of observation, I paid no attention to the black SUV that pulled onto the street from Bouchard's lot as I drove away.

At the front desk of the police station I asked to speak with a cop named Tkatchuk.

"Your name?"

"Max Campbell."

The cop at the desk picked up a phone and spoke quietly into it.

"What is the reason for your visit?" he asked looking up from the phone.

"I have information about some missing women."

He spoke into the phone again, hung up and, hitting a buzzer, nodded toward a door and told me to follow him. I was escorted down a long hallway and into a room with several occupied desks. We walked to a desk in the far back corner, and another young man, who was sitting behind it, got up and stretched out his hand.

"Mr. Campbell have a seat," he said to me. "Thanks, Mike," he said to the cop who was already heading back to the front. I sat down.

"So, you know something about some missing women."

Detective Corporal Tkatchuk was very young. He appeared so young that I would have guessed he was in high school if he wasn't sitting behind a desk with a nameplate. Mind you, I was still having trouble determining the age of anyone under thirty.

"Yeah, it's just something I overheard. I don't know how important it is."

"How did you know to ask for me?"

Good question, I thought. "A guy named Daniel gave me your name."

The detective's eyebrows went up.

"Daniel Bird?"

"Yes." I'd just learned Daniel and his brother's last name when Aaron showed me how to put their contact information into my phone.

"How does someone like you end up chatting with Daniel Bird?"

Good question, I thought. *Wish I had a good answer!* I really didn't want to discuss my relationship with the Bird brothers. "I met him in a Starbucks. He heard me telling a friend what I'd overheard."

"Daniel Bird overheard you telling a friend what you'd overheard." The detective had an understandably skeptical look on his face.

"I just bought the penthouse suite at The Meewasin." It

was best that I jump into the lie I'd intended to tell before the lie I'd just made up got out of hand. "I was waiting to meet the head developer, a guy named Bouchard, and he was talking on his phone, and I guess he didn't realize I could hear him."

Detective Tkatchuk seemed interested again.

"I heard him say, 'Get rid of those girls and get us some new ones.' And then he said, 'The younger, the better,' and then he laughed. It was gall-darned creepy."

The young man across the desk leaned back in his chair, crossed his arms, and stared at me without expression. He suddenly seemed much older. He didn't speak for what felt like several minutes. It was gall-darned creepy.

"Is that all you've got for me, Mr. Campbell?"

I'd expected him to ask more questions, but now he seemed ready to end the conversation.

"I guess that's not much for you to go on," I said, "but someone should look into this Bouchard, don't you think?"

Detective Tkatchuk stared at me some more, then said slowly, "Mr. Campbell, what is it you want?"

"I guess I want to help. I know what I've told you isn't enough for you to arrest Bouchard, but you can look into him, can't you?"

"Actually, that's not really enough for me to even pick up the phone and call the man. Daniel Bird should have known that before he sent you down here."

Well, that floored me. I have to admit, I'd told a pretty lame story on top of doing an awful job of anticipating the questions the detective might ask.

"Detective, I get why it looks like Daniel Bird sent me here," I said, "but I promise you I came of my own accord. I believe that Bouchard is involved in this, and I also believe that you think so too."

He looked at me without expression for a moment.

"You just bought the penthouse suite at The Meewasin?

That must have cost a pretty penny."

"I won a lottery."

"Lucky guy. You are right, Mr. Campbell. Someone does need to do something. Unfortunately, I am the only one assigned to this case, and it's not the only case I'm working on." His smooth brows furrowed. He got up from his desk and said, "Wait here, please."

I watched the detective get up and walk away, and as soon as I felt reasonably confident that he was gone, I looked back to the wall behind his desk. On it was a large cork bulletin board with numerous papers, pictures and business cards posted on it. In the upper right-hand corner was a photo that had caught my attention as I entered the area. It appeared to be the type of picture captured by a security camera of the sort often found in the front entrance of a bank. It was a picture of a young man and a boy. Neither of them was looking up toward the camera, but there was no doubt in my mind that it was Aaron and me.

As I sat looking at the photo, my thoughts went back to that day not so long ago. My new body was barely twenty-four hours old. I'd known the young lad in the picture with me for even less time. I recalled Aaron telling me that I should not look up at the camera in that bank, but he had said that after I had already done so. And yet here was a photo of us that did not show our faces. Could I hope that the camera didn't actually snap a picture of me as I glanced up at it?

About the time that I realized I was staring at the photo as if mesmerized by it I became aware that the detective had returned and was looking at me. I did my best to look away from the image slowly, as if my interest in it was insignificant, and not jump like I'd been caught with my finger up my nose. He stared at me for a moment and then reached into the desk to retrieve a business card from the top drawer.

"I was about to go for a cup of coffee, Mr. Campbell. Join me?"

"Sure," I said, not trying to mask the surprise in my voice, and following him out onto the street. We headed east on foot. Neither of us spoke until we had put a block between ourselves and the station.

"That's you in the photo, isn't it?" The detective said.

CHAPTER TWELVE

It was a statement as much as a question. I felt a slight burst of panic in my chest, and my knees may have wobbled ever so slightly.

Detective Tkatchuk was an average built man, about five feet ten inches tall. He had a quality about him that made him seem lighter than he probably was. It may have been the confident way he carried himself or possibly the youthful spring in his step. Despite his apparent youth, his demeanour commanded respect, probably the result of his police training. When I didn't respond, he continued.

"I get the impression from you that you genuinely want to help. Am I wrong Mr. Campbell?"

"Yes, I guess I do. Something has to be done."

"Then perhaps you can help me by freeing up some of my time, by helping me solve another case I've been assigned. You see, I have the good fortune to be kind of a case-file trash-can for the department. For reasons I won't get into, I was promoted to my position to fill a political need and not a departmental one, and as a result, instead of being assigned only murder cases or theft cases, I get tossed every case that no one else wants to deal with."

We had arrived at a small coffee shop on 1st Avenue where we each purchased coffee to go and sat at one of two empty street-side tables.

"So, Mr. Campbell, one case I've been working on for a few weeks involves the death of an old man on a highway just outside of town. The accident wasn't so unusual. The old guy should have had his license revoked years ago. What brought it to our attention was a number of withdrawals made from the guy's bank accounts around the time of his death."

Despite the mild panic I was feeling at the direction this conversation was going, I couldn't help but be a little pissed about his assumption that I shouldn't have been driving. I was a good driver!

"There were only four transactions on the cards, but a sizable amount of money was withdrawn. The only information I've had to go on is a couple of security camera images that were taken at the time of the withdrawals. Unless a person is already in our files, our facial recognition software can't do much to find a person from a couple of low-res photos, so needless to say, I wasn't getting very far on the case." The detective looked me straight in the eyes as he continued. "Imagine my surprise when the man in the photos walked up to my desk this morning."

I managed to not break eye contact with him. We both just sat there quietly and waited. He was waiting to see how I would respond. I was waiting to see if my heart was going to start beating again. It took a considerable force of will to keep my voice from quavering when I finally did respond.

"Are you saying you think I had something to do with some old man's death?" I managed to conjure a tone of incredulity.

The Detective said nothing, just took a small sip of his coffee and waited.

"I don't know what to tell you," I said. "I don't know anything about any old man."

With that, I decided I'd said enough. Now that my heart had resumed a semblance of its regular rhythm I could wait in silence as well.

"Not the death, Mr. Campbell, just the money."

"Just Max," I said. "If I was the kind of guy who steals money would I also be the kind of person who stops by the police station and offers to help with an investigation?"

"That thought had crossed my mind, Max. I've always been a good judge of character, and you don't strike me as being a bad person, so if you tell me you had nothing to do with this old man, I'm inclined to believe you."

"I guess I could have been in that bank, but trust me, I would have been taking money from my own account," I said, truthfully.

"I haven't heard anything from the old man's daughter for almost two weeks, so If I don't do anything, the case will likely get filed. She doesn't look like she's going to miss the money anyway."

My daughter Connie and her husband had done very well for themselves, and she likes to dress so that everyone knows it. Connie has never been a greedy person, but she's always had a strong sense of justice. She wouldn't be worried about the money, but she would be rankled that someone might have committed a crime against her family, and worse, gotten away with it.

"So, about Bouchard?" I prodded, wanting to get back to my reason for being there.

"As you can probably imagine, missing First Nations girls is another case that nobody wanted. With all the shit in the news about 'Missing and Murdered Indigenous Women and Girls, you would think the entire department would be working on it, but there's just me. That isn't to say I don't want it. I do. The problem with investigating a case like this is that people think it's some issue that happened at some time in the past. No one seems to realize its a problem that going on right now. People talk as if it can all be made better by forming committees and holding hands. All that seems to do is deflect the public's attention from what's still going on. And it's not just going on here in Saskatoon. It's happening all over North America."

Detective Tkatchuk's previous professional bearing was gone and the passion he had for his job, or more specifically this case, was evident on his face and in his voice. He leaned toward me across the table.

"Do you mind if I ask how much you won?"

His sudden change of topic left my brain hanging in the middle of nowhere for a couple of seconds.

"Over forty million," I answered when what he had asked finally registered.

"Wow. I'm tempted to ask you for a loan."

"You wouldn't be the first."

"I really have no right to ask this of you, in fact, I'd be in a load of shit if anyone found out I did, but I need help on this. It's been made clear to me that there's no money in the budget to get me any help. Am I right in thinking that spending a little money isn't going to bother you very much, Max?"

"I came here because I want to help. To be honest, winning the lottery has left me feeling a little lost. If helping you with this gives my life a little purpose, I'm all in. But I have to tell you that I have no idea where to begin."

"Let's start with that Son-of-a-bitch, Bouchard. Getting on his case is something you can do that I can't."

His excitement was contagious, and we were now leaning across the table like we were going to arm wrestle. He again seemed much too young to be a cop let alone one with the responsibility he'd been handed.

"As you probably already know," He continued, "Henry Bouchard moved to Saskatoon from Montreal less than three years ago. He timed his move very well to take advantage of our little economic boom. Even with that considered, he seems to have become a big man in the city's business community in a remarkable short time. Too short, in my opinion, to have made so many contacts and to have as much influence as he does."

I already liked where this seemed to be going.

"When Daniel Bird came to me and told me he thought that Bouchard might be involved in these missing girls I wanted to believe him. It was the first lead of any sort that I'd had in the case. I went to speak with Bouchard. He acted like he was mildly offended that someone as unimportant as me would dare to waste his time. He as much as told me so. He then had the gall to have one of his men show me out. Not two hours later my Sergeant told me to lay off Bouchard.

"There is an arrogance about that man. He thinks he is above the law. That, and the fact that he's the most unlikeable prick I've ever met, makes me hope that he's involved in *something* we can lock him up for."

"Well, at least I'm sure we're talking about the same guy," I said.

Corporal Tkatchuk paused and looked very directly into my eyes.

"For all I know, the Bird brothers may be paying you to tell me this shit you 'overheard'. For all I know, I may have lost my fucking mind, but for some reason, I do believe that you really want to help. And, for some reason, I trust you. So, tell me Mr. Campbell, am I crazy?"

"I want to help."

"Good to know, Mr. Campbell. Bouchard was a successful businessman in Montreal before coming to Saskatoon. I suspect that there was more to his decision to move here than just our little boom. It stands to reason that there are people in Montreal who know things about this guy. If the powers that sign my cheques really wanted me to do my job, I'd still be looking into this bastard, and I'd be flying to Montreal to do it, but that isn't the case."

He paused.

Taking my cue, I said, "Well, I haven't been out east in a long time. I guess I'm going to Montreal."

Tkatchuk smiled broadly.

"Hopefully, buy poking around a bit, you'll be able to dig up some shit on this guy that I can use to give me some leverage. Something I can show my superiors to prove that I have to look into this guy. I know this is a lot to ask of you, Max…"

"No, really, I want to do what I can. I'm serious when I say I want to help."

"Start with the Real Estate and construction people. Ask around. Somebody out there is bound to have some dirt on this asshole."

The detective took a business card out of his shirt pocket. It was a standard issue Saskatoon Police business card, as far as I could tell, and it read Corporal Corey Tkatchuk. 'Detective' was typed on the line below with an office number and cell phone number on the bottom right-hand corner.

We got up from the table as Corey continued, "Keep me posted while you're out there and be careful, Max. It can be dangerous when you start poking around where you aren't welcome."

I felt pretty good as I walked back to my truck. While it was true that I didn't know exactly what I was doing, at least I was doing something.

Once back in my truck, I called Air Canada and booked a flight to Montreal for that evening. I even managed to get my new cell phone to find the number for me. Look at me! Almost as smart as the average five-year-old.

I was as excited as a schoolgirl at her first dance on the drive back to the apartment. With every new experience, the feeling that my new life had a particular purpose was intensified. I couldn't wait to talk to Aaron, not just about my upcoming trip, but to see if his friend had been able to find out anything.

I had just pulled into my parking spot at the rear of the building when I heard the high-pitched screeching of tires on pavement. I jumped quickly out of the truck, thinking there may have been an accident in the alley behind me. The site that greeted me was of no accident, but rather that of two large and very ugly men exiting an SUV that had stopped right behind my truck. Both men moved quickly toward me.

"Hi, guys! What can I do...?" That was all I got out before the first one to reach me slammed his hands into my chest and pushed.

CHAPTER THIRTEEN

I almost went down, but managed to get my feet back under me, thanks, no doubt, to all the rugby practice.

"What the heck, guys?" I said.

"Monsieur Bouchard does not like people embarrassing him."

His French accent was so strong that I wasn't entirely sure I understood him.

The other guy moved behind me to block my retreat. I wasn't retreating. The talking, pushing guy stepped toward me again, and suddenly my heart was racing. These guys were seriously going to hurt me!

"Hey, I…" I began.

"He doesn't like people snooping either."

They were both huskier than me and looked like they'd made a career of fighting. By contrast, over the course of two lifetimes, I'd been in one fight, and it only lasted about two seconds. I was worried. Heck, I was scared! I was trying to determine if I had any options when the talkative guy began a lunge like he was going to push me again, right into the arms of his silent friend behind me.

And that's when it all got very weird!

No sooner had the talkative guy begun his lunge when he suddenly started moving in slow motion. It was indescribably, unbelievably strange! One minute he was moving very fast for a guy his size and the next minute he looked as though he was swimming through molasses. Before I had a chance to register what was happening my adrenaline-charged reflexes kicked into action, and I swung my left arm, knocking both of his arms aside, and with my right fist, I gave him a quick punch to the side of his head. Spinning and ducking down I gave his quiet friend a solid punch in the abdomen. The first man was falling to the pavement like he had tripped during a walk on the moon. That was what came to mind. They were moving like the Apollo astronauts moved on the moon.

I stepped aside and straightened in time to see Mr. Talkative slowly hit the ground. Releasing a breath I was holding, I turned again to see his friend suddenly fly backward, landing first on his backside and then doing a reverse somersault to end up face down on the asphalt. His painful looking acrobatics appeared to happen at normal speed.

What the heck just happened? I asked myself. *That was crazy!*

Both men were getting up slowly, and the pushy guy was screaming at me, but his words made no sense. Over the years I'd picked up a little bit of French, but I could understand it only if it was spoken very slowly. He was definitely not speaking slowly, and what he was saying wasn't anything I was familiar with. Again, they both began to move toward me, the silent fellow holding an arm across his abdomen and Mr. Pushy rubbing the side of his head, and each of them looking very, very angry.

I took a couple of steps backward thinking it would give me some time to decide what I should do. And suddenly, they were both doing the moonwalk thing again.

Holy Cow! Either they're moving very slowly, or I'm moving very fast!

I stepped to the side and slipped in behind both men. They didn't seem to notice I was no longer in front of them. The talking man's voice became much deeper and drawled like a record playing at the wrong speed. I stepped up between them, and with a hand on each of their backs, I gave them a push in the direction they were going. And then suddenly the two of them flew forward, slamming into their SUV with a force that nearly rocked the vehicle onto two wheels. The sound of them hitting it was like a crack of thunder.

Holy Cow! I thought. *I've got Super Speed!*

Unbelievably, the two men were getting up off the ground from where they had fallen. They were definitely tough guys. I thought I might have killed them both. Without even looking at each other they both moved to get back in their dented vehicle. Each had decided, independent of the other, that they were not sticking around to have another go at me. I watched as the SUV sped away.

I stood in the parking lot for several minutes after they left. I would have believed that little could surprise me, after being reborn and finding I had the ability to see people's future, but this had me completely stupefied.

What in the name of all things holy is going on? Have I gone completely nuts?

I wasn't likely to find an answer to my first question by standing in the parking lot and staring down the lane. I suspected there might be a simple, three-letter answer to the second question.

Once again, I was excited to talk to…

"Aaron!" I called upon entering the suite.

There was no answer.

"Aaron."

Nothing.

I knocked on Aaron's bedroom door. No answer. For the first time since moving in, I opened the door to his room and looked in. I had to be sure that he wasn't sleeping. He wasn't sleeping.

Tarnation! Where is that kid?

I wrote a note telling him where I was going and that I'd be back soon. I hate to admit it, but in all the strange goings-on, I'd forgotten I could send him a text or, for that matter, give him a call.

I tossed a spare shirt and shaving gear into my gym bag and headed to the airport.

I spent the entire flight to Montreal reliving the fight I'd had with Bouchard's thugs. The more I thought about it, the more I was certain I'd been gifted with some kind of super speed. After all, it wouldn't make sense for those two guys to start moving extra slow just to give me a chance. They didn't seem like the type. And the way they flew into their SUV when I pushed them, and practically knocked it over when they hit it. That was crazy! But no matter how much I pondered it I had no more answers as to where such an ability had come from than I knew how I'd been reborn and gained the power of precognition. I had a strong urge to get up from my seat and see how fast I could run to the front of the plane and back again. I restrained myself. There was no telling what the physical repercussions of testing my speed on an aircraft in flight might be. In moving as fast as I did during the fight, I seemed to be defying the laws of physics. While I was several thousand feet above the earth, it might be best to leave those laws the way they were.

The next morning, I found myself in a rented Ford F150, heading for Montreal's downtown core in search of construction sites. Having spent most of my new life working in construction, I felt I could communicate with the tradesmen at any work site and stay well within my comfort zone. It was a good way to ease in to this investigation thing.

As I neared the downtown, I was struck by the apparent age and the sheer grandeur of the city. The oldest buildings you see in the Canadian Prairies are never much more than a hundred years old, and most are much younger. By contrast, the city of Montreal is more than three times that old, three hundred years during which Montrealer's have taken particular pride in their city's architectural distinctiveness.

As I turned right on Avenue Union, I was struck again with a realization I'd had in the airport the previous evening; Montreal women are quite possibly another form of human life. Not only are many of them absurdly attractive, but they also have a sense of style you won't find anywhere else on the continent. At nine-thirty in the morning, the downtown streets were teaming with pedestrians, many of them young ladies, and I wondered why they even allowed men to drive those streets. Distracted driving takes on a whole new meaning in this town. Then I spotted what appeared to be a bag lady pushing a shopping cart loaded with junk and concluded that Montreal's destitute dress better than most Canadian politicians.

As luck would have it, I found my first construction site in time for the morning coffee break. From the street I could see many of the construction workers sitting, drinking coffee and smoking. I was asking for trouble walking on to a work site without a hard hat, but having no other option, I took a deep breath and strode in like I belonged. Five guys were sitting at a picnic table not far from the gate. I walked over to them.

"Hi, guys!" I said. *Cripes, I hope they speak English.*

A couple of the guys looked up. One of them nodded.

"Mind if I ask you guys a couple of questions?"

The one that had nodded held eye contact with me, so I sat down across from him.

"Ask away," he said. Good clear English.

"I'm from Saskatoon, and I'm looking for work."

"I thought Saskatoon was booming." It was one of the guys

on my side of the table.

"Yeah, but my wife is getting transferred, so here I am. Is anyone around here looking for help?"

"What do you do?" the man across from me asked. I'd learned in my short time working with them that tradespeople are generally pretty friendly. Moving from one job site to the next, as one project ended and the next began, gave them alot of practice meeting new people and making friends. These guys were just like the those I worked with in Saskatoon, and the conversation was already starting to flow nicely.

"Carpenter," I lied.

"Not much for Carpenters," said the same voice from my side of the table.

"Yeah. Lots of Carpenters looking for work right now," said the man across from me. "But some new jobs are coming up. The work at the General is starting soon."

"Is that the hospital?" I asked.

"Oui, it's going to be a big job, that one," the guy on my side said. His accent was a little thicker.

"I heard Bouchard has something starting soon," I said.

"What? I thought that son-of-a-bitch was out in your town," My Side said.

"You don't like Bouchard?" I asked looking at the man on my side.

"No one likes Bouchard. No one was sad to see him leave town." This was the guy across from me.

"What's so bad about Bouchard?"

"Bouchard is a fucking creepy bastard," Across said. "And if he can find a reason not to pay, he doesn't pay, let me tell you."

The other men started to talk amongst themselves, and My Side got up and came over to our end of the table but didn't sit down.

"I hate guys like that," I said.

"He's worse than that. People who cross that man get hurt."

"What?" I asked, faking surprise. "I have friends who are working for him!"

"Tell them to be careful with that guy. They piss him off, they could end up like Pierre."

"We don't know for sure about Pierre," Across said.

"Pierre was at the wrong place at the wrong time, and Bouchard didn't like it. Now Pierre's a cripple, eh?"

"What? My friends need to know if they should watch out for this guy," I said, speaking fast because the men were getting up to go back to work. "Could I talk to this Pierre?"

My Side pulled out his phone and quickly rattled off a number, then was patient enough to repeat it after I fumbled with my device like I had never used it before. I left the site feeling quite proud of myself.

It turned out that Pierre Bernard spoke English without an accent, something I was delighted to hear on the phone. At first, he didn't seem interested in talking with me, so I tried a tactic that I recommend in any situation of this sort; I begged. Forty-five minutes later I was pulling up in front of Pierre's house.

"Come in!" The voice sounded like it was coming from deep inside the house, so I opened the door and went looking for it. I found Pierre in a small room toward the back. He was in a wheelchair.

"Thank you for seeing me. It means a lot to me."

"Sit down. Coke? It's all I can offer you," Pierre said. He reached into a cooler next to his chair and pulled out a coke. It looked cold.

"Sure. Thanks."

"So why are you so interested in talking to me about my accident?" Pierre got straight to the point.

"The guys downtown implied it wasn't an accident," I

replied.

"It wasn't a fucking accident," Pierre said strongly. "But no one wants to believe me."

"What happened?"

"Why do you want to know? What is it to you?"

Again, honesty was the best policy. It stood to reason that Pierre would have no love for Bouchard.

"I need to know because he's moved to my city and I have reason to believe he is up to no good."

"Bouchard is an evil bastard. Stay away from that man. You don't want to tangle with him."

"Girls in our city have gone missing."

"Fuck." For a moment, Pierre actually looked as if he was going to cry, and I imagined what it might be like to deal with such an utterly frustrating situation. He, too, knew something about Bouchard that he could not prove, but he had been dealing with it for a lot longer than me. Even worse, his knowledge had put him in a wheelchair.

"I could really use your help. I'm working kind of informally with the only cop in Saskatoon that's been assigned to look into it. It would be helpful if you could tell me what you know."

"I was working on a condo that Bouchard was building," Pierre said quietly. "I'm an electrician. We only had a couple of units to finish up. I decided to go back to work one Friday evening because I didn't have anything better to do. My wife and I had just separated, and I was better off working than sitting around moping." He paused for a bit. "When I got there, I found the lights were on in some of the main floor rooms. It seemed odd, so I went in to see what was going on. I walked in on some guys having a party with some young women that looked like they could be hookers. Pretty young, a lot of them. I tried to back out of the room hoping that no one noticed me and back right into Bouchard. He was pretty pissed and had his goons throw me out after telling me to keep my mouth shut. Funny thing was, if they hadn't roughed me up, I probably would never have mentioned it to anyone. But I never liked that bastard, and I didn't like being pushed around, so I went to the police. It was probably the stupidest thing I've ever done. Who gives a shit if a rich guy likes young hookers? Monday night while I was leaving work a car came around the corner. They called it a hit and run."

"What makes you so sure it wasn't?" As soon as I said it, I knew I could have phrased it better.

"Because I saw the fucker that was driving the fucking car!" Pierre screamed at me. "It was one of the bastards that threw me out of their little party."

"I'm sorry. I wasn't doubting you," I said.

"The police came to see me in the hospital," Pierre continued quietly. "They asked if I saw the driver. When I told them that, not only did I see him, but I knew who the man was and who he worked for, they stopped taking notes and headed for the door, saying they would look into it. They never got back to me. I was in the hospital for two months and called those guys several times, but they never returned my calls.

"A few weeks later I got a call from a different cop, an RCMP. He came by and talked to me about my accident. He seemed more sincere when he said he'd be in touch, but I never heard from him again either. So here I sit. Thank God I got insurance, or I'd be fucked." He looked down at his legs. "I mean, even more fucked."

He was silent for a moment, so I asked him if he had the name of the RCMP officer.

"On that stand over there."

I got up from my seat and noticed the unopened can of Coke in my hand. I made to hand it back to him, but he said, "Keep it."

I found the business card on the stand and was about to ask for paper to copy the information. Pierre anticipated my need and said, "Just take a picture of it."

"I can do that," I responded with a little more enthusiasm than I intended.

I thanked him for his help, and the Coke, and headed back out to the truck.

"Tremblay." The voice was raspy.

"Detective Tremblay? My name is Max Campbell. I'm here visiting from Saskatoon, and I'm wondering if you might have time to meet with me. I would like to ask you a few questions about Henry Bouchard."

There was a long pause on the other end of the line, and then the voice continued at a slightly lower pitch.

"Saskatoon, you say. What can I tell you about Mr. Bouchard?"

"I know it's an imposition, but I would really appreciate it if you could meet with me."

Another pause.

"Where are you now Mr. Campbell?"

I told him.

"There's a good restaurant not far from there. I could be there in about twenty minutes. We could grab a bite to eat. I haven't had lunch yet."

I suddenly realized I was famished.

Detective Tremblay looked the way he sounded, with his dry grey skin and steel wool hair.

"Thank you for meeting me. It's very much appreciated," I said as I reached for his hand. Immediately there was the familiar white flash.

***

I was seated behind a desk, and there was a fat man in a doorway yelling at me. I was yelling back. It was an unusual experience because I was being screamed at in French and I was screaming back in French, and through the entire exchange I made out only one word. Bouchard.

The fat man in the doorway threw his hands in the air in apparent frustration, pointed at me, yelled a bit more, then grabbed the doorknob and slammed the door shut behind him.

***

"So, who are you, Mr. Campbell, that I should be sharing information with you."

"Like I told you on the phone, I'm here from Saskatoon. I came to Montreal to see what I could find out about Henry Bouchard."

"That doesn't answer my question, Mr. Campbell. Who are you?"

Reasonable question.

"I am working, informally, with a young detective on the Saskatoon Police Force named Tkatchuk. I wish I could tell you that I had some authority to be here asking you questions, but the truth is, I'm just a guy who's trying to help. You see, some young women in our city have gone missing in the last couple of years and Corporal Tkatchuk is the only cop that has been assigned to their case."

"I see."

"He feels that he has been hung out to dry, so to speak. It is as if his superiors in the force don't actually want him to do his job."

Tremblay's eyebrows went up, and he nodded slightly.

"And Bouchard?"

"There are some people in Saskatoon, myself and Tkatchuk included, who believe that Henry Bouchard is involved in some way." I tried to give the name its French pronunciation. Tremblay winced.

"How did you find me?"

I told him how I had spent my morning.

"You had a very productive morning, Mr. Campbell. It is not usually that easy. Maybe it helps that you look like that superhero, or at least the actor who plays the superhero."

"I get that a lot."

"What is the name of the Corporal in Saskatoon? I believe I would like to speak with him."

I pulled out Corporal Tkatchuk's card out of my pocket and gave it to him. I had already entered the information into my phone.

"So, you believed Pierre's story," I said.

"I had met Henry Bouchard some time before I first spoke with Mr. Bernard. My wife and I attended a wedding, and at the dinner we were, how can I say it, lucky enough to get to sit with Bouchard. I found him to be an extremely unlikeable man. When Mr. Bernard told me his story, I did not find it that hard to believe."

"Why has nothing been done about it?" I asked.

"I tried. I know that sounds terrible. I spoke to my Sergeant to let him know I wanted to speak with Bouchard about his activities. He told me that the story from one man was not a good enough reason to bother a prominent citizen like Henry Bouchard. We argued about it but rank prevailed. As I'm sure he told you, Mr. Bernard recognized the man driving the vehicle that hit him. Knew him to be employed by Bouchard. So, I searched our files and those files I could access from the city force. I found that Bouchard's name came up surprisingly often for a man of his 'professional standing'." Detective Tremblay used air-quotes to emphasize 'Professional Standing'. "But despite having fingers pointed at him so often, no one has ever put any time into investigating him. As much as it troubles me to consider how such a thing could be, I am forced to believe that Henry Bouchard has 'friends' on both the city police force and the RCMP. I do not know how he does it, but Henry Bouchard has a way of gaining the loyalty of significant people. Have you met him, Mr. Campbell?"

The memory of the precognitive flash I had with Bouchard imposed itself on me, and I shuddered.

"Exactly, Mr. Campbell. How is it that an obnoxious asshole like him has managed to make connections with anyone, let alone the big movers and shakers in a city like Montreal?"

"He seems to be doing the same thing in Saskatoon. Somehow, he has insinuated himself into the Saskatoon business community, and he's done it very quickly." I wanted to tell him what I knew, but I could not tell him how I knew it, so I let him go on.

"I wanted very much to shut Bouchard down. I wanted to put him out of business. I wanted to put him in prison where I very strongly believe he belongs, but I have been stopped at every turn by the very people who should be helping me to make it happen. I have tried multiple approaches in the hopes of getting around the roadblocks they put up in front of me, but I am only one cop. And, I'm sorry, Mr. Campbell, but I need my job. Most days I even like my job. But I will tell you something I believe very strongly. If you care about the people in your city, Mr. Campbell, you should be there doing everything you can to stop that man from hurting them. I believe that Henry Bouchard hurts people, and enjoys doing it."

I suddenly had a sick feeling in the pit of my stomach that took all the enjoyment out of an excellent meal.

"I think I will head back to Saskatoon," I said.

"You should. I will continue to do what I can, but so far, that has not been very much. And I will get in touch with this Detective Corporal Tkatchuk of yours. But if Bouchard has made the same kind of contacts in Saskatoon as he did here in Montreal, it might be that the only one who can stop him is someone who is working without the 'authority' to do so. Someone like you, Mr. Campbell. But be careful. Henry Bouchard is a very dangerous man."

I thanked him and paid for our meals. I didn't bother to warn him that he was about to have another confrontation with his sergeant.

I still had the sick feeling in my stomach when I got back into the truck, so I pulled out my iPhone and tapped on the icon for Aaron. He didn't answer.

I was on the three-fifteen WestJet flight back to Saskatoon.

CHAPTER FOURTEEN

I tried calling Aaron again as soon as I was off the plane. There was still no answer, so I took a chance that I'd find Matthew at his Starbucks office and drove downtown.

I was parking in front of the coffee shop when I saw a man in a wheelchair coming out. I honked to get his attention, and he waited for me.

"Orville," Matthew said as I approached.

"Matthew, have you seen Aaron?" I didn't feel like wasting any time with pleasantries.

"No. Not in a couple days."

"Cripes!" I said. "He was going to have a friend check out Bouchard's nightclub. That was the night before last. I haven't heard from him since. And he's not answering his phone."

Matthew gave me a look that was one part grimace, and four parts intense study of my soul. What was it about this guy? Even without his disability he wouldn't have had the physical presence of his extremely fit brother, and yet here he was, in a wheelchair, with legs that had atrophied to the size of matchsticks, and somehow, he made me feel insignificant.

"Has Aaron ever been gone like this before?"

"Never for more than one night," I responded.

Matthew looked concerned.

"It is not in Aaron's nature to go looking for trouble, but," Matthew paused as his face took on a slightly pained expression, "his feelings toward you may have made him take risks he wouldn't normally take. I can make some calls to see if Aaron has been seen, but I think that it's time someone checks out what's going on at WonderWall."

"I can do that," I said.

"I could ask Daniel to send some of his guys with you if you like, but that hasn't really worked in the past."

"I can check the place out on my own," I said.

"I'll ask Daniel to get his guys looking for Aaron if no one has seen him."

"Good. Thanks." I turned to go.

"And Orville…"

I turned back as Matthew continued.

"I don't believe you realize how uniquely two-spirited our young Aaron is. Much like yourself. I believe it's important that you take the time to talk about that, the next time the two of you have an opportunity. You mean too much to each other to keep such important secrets."

The hair on every part of my body stood up as a slight chill swept over me. I've met many people over the years who seem to have an understanding of the world that is deeper than what most of us have, but this guy takes the cake. Somehow, he gives the impression he knows things about *me* that no one could possibly know.

I hopped out of the truck with butterflies trying to fight their way out of my stomach. I was about to do something I hadn't done in over seventy years. In fact, it was something I'd only ever done three times in my entire life.

'I hope you're okay with this, Elsie?'

'Don't be silly, my silly man!' I heard my late wife's voice like she was walking next to me. *'You should live your new life to the fullest. Besides, you must do everything you can to help these young people.'*

I took a deep breath and opened the door to the bar.

Demi smiled when she saw me and made my heart jump into my throat.

Dang, this girl is pretty.

"Max!"

"Hi, Demi! How are you?"

"I'm good! Where've you been? We haven't seen you all week."

The Colonial had become something of a hangout for me, and I often dragged the guys on the Rugby team here after games.

"I've been a little busy. Say, Demi, are you working this evening?"

"I'm done as soon as the dinner rush slows down," she said with a look of excited anticipation on her face."

"I was wondering if you'd be interested in going to WonderWall with me tonight?"

"I'd love to!" She almost shouted it and then immediately looked embarrassed.

We exchanged our cell numbers, and I asked her to text me her address.

"I'll see you tonight," I said. "What time should I pick you up?"

"Ten-ish? I'll text you when I'm off to confirm."

She grabbed me and gave me a quick hug. There was a white flash.

***

I was in a large, loud room with flashing lights and a crowd of young people jostling and gyrating. I was sitting at a tall table on a tall chair and holding a beer in my delicate hand. I was craning my neck to see over the crowd into the far reaches of the room. I could feel myself getting very, very angry.

***

And then I was back, looking into the dazzling eyes of my first first-date in seventy years, and I knew that at some point in the evening, she was going to feel quite differently about me than she did as I turned to leave.

I had donned a new t-shirt and jeans and felt I looked pretty good. The second she opened the door, I knew I should have tried much harder. She was absolutely stunning, and I was absolutely stunned. As we walked to the stairs, I consoled myself in the knowledge that no one was going to be looking at me.

This girl knew how to dress. Her makeup and hair were perfectly done to accent her big beautiful eyes. Her thin-strapped silky top perfectly accentuated what it was designed to accent, and her high-heeled shoes and tiny little skirt, that looked to me like little more than a wide belt, made her remarkably toned legs look unbelievably long.

'Help me, Elsie! I can't even look at her!'

'You're loving every minute of this, and you know it, you old goat!'

Elsie knew me better than anyone, and I was fortunate she never had a jealous bone in her body. It came from her unshakeable confidence. She was well aware of the value she brought to a relationship and was never threatened by other women. She didn't even mind if I admired another good-looking woman now and then, provided I used discretion and didn't embarrass her.

When we got to the truck, I opened the door for her, offering her my hand to help her into the cab. She gave me a smile that caused every ounce of blood in my body to race up to my face to look at her. I had to take several calming breaths to slow my racing heart as I walked around to my side of the truck.

I think I managed to keep up my end of the conversation on the way to the nightclub. I wanted to be as nice as possible to this beautiful young woman, if only to increase the chances that she would forgive me for abandoning her, as the earlier flash had told me I would do at some point during the evening. She was a lovely girl, and I got the impression that she felt quite strongly about me. She didn't deserve to have me use her or mislead her as to my intentions.

I was right in my prediction. No one looked at me as we joined the lineup outside the nightclub. Even the other girls looked at Demi, with mixed admiration and jealousy, before noticing that I was next to her. Other guys were outright gawking at her and getting punches and jabs in the ribs from their companions as a result. None of those young ladies were the quality of my Elsie or my new date.

Once inside, I gave myself a few seconds to get oriented and to adjust to the level of noise in the cavernous room. When I'd managed to merge my surroundings to the memory of my earlier flash, I bellowed in Demi's ear that we might find a table toward the far right side of the room. Finding a table as it was being abandoned made Demi give me another one of her mind-blowing smiles. My face felt warm as I held her chair.

I wanted badly to go searching the place as soon as we had our drinks ordered, but before I had a chance to slip away, Demi grabbed my hand and dragged me out on the dance floor. I let myself get pulled along in part because I wanted Demi to have some fun this evening, but also, I must admit, because I really wanted to watch this girl dance. I wasn't disappointed. Never have I felt anything but self-conscious embarrassment when on a dance floor. This evening, I was so taken up by the vision in front of me, I didn't give a single thought to what *my* feet were doing.

After a couple of dances, Demi grew tired of being watched by everyone around her and took my hand to lead me back to our table. The waitress was dropping off our drinks, and I handed her two twenty-dollar bills, telling her to keep the change. She gave me her brightest smile, but sadly, it dimmed in comparison to Demi's.

I once again held the chair for her, and she gave me a quick kiss on the cheek in thanks. It had the same blood-flow-altering effect that she had on me the first day we met, but the pressure went away as soon as I thought about what I was planning to do next.

"I've got to go find a washroom," I yelled in Demi's ear. I didn't think I could possibly cause more damage to her eardrum than the pounding music was already doing.

I turned away from her before she had a chance to point me in the right direction. I wanted to check out a hallway I'd spotted in a far corner of the room, and I didn't think I was going to find the men's washroom there. The hallway was blocked by two guys, each almost as large as my friend Kyle. I couldn't imagine what the bouncers could be guarding in the back of that nightclub, and for that reason, more than any, I wanted to find out.

This speed thing better work or I'm about to get my butt kicked.

I walked toward the two big brutes. Both men stood with their arms crossed in that stance of defiance that dares anyone to challenge them. When they noticed me coming toward them, they straightened up and tensed their arms, and they both appeared to grow a couple of feet taller. I felt my heart begin to race as I focused on moving toward them as fast as I could. The pounding music did that weird slowing down thing that reminded me of a record being played on the wrong speed, and when I reached the bouncers, I slapped them each on the side of their heads. My palms stung like I'd spanked a granite wall, but the effect on the two bruisers looked decidedly more painful. Their heads slammed together with a 'whunk' sound that was strangely well timed to the slow thumping beat of the music. They crumpled to the floor.

Holy Cow! That's really going to hurt when they wake up! I thought.

I was reasonably sure that they would wake up, but really had no way of judging the actual force with which I had struck them.

The short hallway had a door on each side that appeared to be closets or storage rooms, but I couldn't be sure as both doors were locked. I moved on to where the corridor turned to the left. Rounding the corner, I found another man guarding a doorway at the end of a short hall. We spotted each other simultaneously, and the music slowed as I punched him in the solar plexus. Stepping over him I opened the door to a nightmare.

Dim red lights illuminated a room that looked disgustingly familiar. There were couches and pillows scattered around and small mattresses laying on the floor. Young, half-naked girls were in the grips of half-naked men. A fully clothed woman had a camcorder pointed at a couple engaged in relations that, if I had my way, would soon put one of them in prison.

Continuing to scan the scene, my eyes fell on another young woman who sat on a couch in one corner of the room. Her arms appeared to be tied behind her back. Her head came up slowly, and she repeatedly blinked as her eyes attempted to focus on me.

"Orville!" she mumbled.

To say I was stunned to hear my real name would be a tremendous understatement. I stared at the young woman in utter astonishment as my baffled brain tried to make a connection. She was tiny, with short dark hair and slight build. She was naked but for a sheer lace bra and panties. Her face was covered in thickly applied makeup which was smeared as if by tears. *She looks like a young Audrey Hepburn,* I thought as I struggled to identify her. Just then she spoke again, her voice slurred and unsteady.

"Max! I knew you'd come!"

As the identity of the pretty young woman slowly hit me, something more substantial did as well, and the world went dark.

I returned to consciousness in the same red room. A pounding in my temples was out of sync with the pounding music from the nightclub down the hall. The room must have been quite well insulated, because the deafening music was reduced to little more than heavy bass notes. Fortunately, my wits returned quickly enough to keep me from opening my eyes fully, thereby alerting everyone in the room to my condition.

I cracked my eyes open just enough to get a fuzzy impression of who was in the room and what they were doing. Fortunately, I had fallen, or been dropped, to one side of the room and facing out, so I was able to see most of the space without having to move my head. Unfortunately, the people I didn't want aware I was awake were standing right in front of me, looking at me as they talked in low voices. One was the woman with the camcorder, another looked like the man I'd punched outside the room. The third was larger and dwarfed the first two. Beyond them, I could see some of the half-naked people standing or sitting and generally looking dazed. I tried to focus on what my captors were saying. The effort made my head hurt.

"...and get them out the back door," the woman with the camcorder was saying. "Haul him out before he wakes up and dispose of him."

I would have no time to devise a fancy plan.

Watch over me, Elsie! I thought, as I pushed myself off the floor and at the same time pushed at the universe to slow the pounding bass from the other room. My head felt like it might explode, but it worked. The music slowed.

Throwing myself across the room, I again punched the man who had been guarding the door. This time I put more energy into it and hit him a little higher, right where his breastbone protected his heart. Not waiting to see the result, I turned and chopped at the neck of the other man. That man, one of the bouncers who had guarded the hall, had managed to start raising his arm, possibly in an attempt to hit me. As a result, my intended blow bounced off of his shoulder and ended up striking him in the side of the head. The pain that flared up in my wrist almost, but not quite, overcame the ache in my head. I slapped Video Woman in the side of the head and stepped past her in one motion. One of the half-naked men had begun moving in the direction of a back door, so I lashed out with my right foot in a kick that caught him in the right shoulder. I slapped two other underdressed guys in the head for good measure, and then relaxed the mental effort that gave me my extra speed. The beat of the muffled music resumed its regular cadence.

Turning, I surveyed the results of my efforts. The bouncers were crumpled on the floor where they had been standing, and video woman had been knocked across the room to lie against a closet door.

"Max! You're so fucking fast!" The words were slurred.

I turned to look at Aaron. The room spun a bit, and I felt faint. It might have been the after effect of a blow to the back of the head. It might also have been the shock of learning my tiny friend and roommate was actually a pretty little modern-day version of my all-time favourite actress.

'Aaron's a girl! I don't understand anything in this crazy world, Elsie!' I thought.

Aaron wiggled herself up off the couch and came up to press herself against me in a strange effort to hug without using her arms, which were tied behind her back. The slow and dreamy quality of her movements told me that she had been drugged. I reached over her and untied her hands. She threw her arms up and around my neck as I picked her up and hugged her to me, unbelievably fighting back tears that threatened to run down my cheeks.

Holding Aaron in my arms, I turned to look at the other girls who had gathered on a couch in the corner. One of the girls was as naked as Aaron, and the others wore even less, so I tossed them blankets from the floor and told them to cover themselves up. I then grabbed another blanket and wrapped it around myself and Aaron, who had her legs around me, clinging like a little monkey.

"We're leaving," I said to the girls as I began to herd them out the door. They all seemed drugged to some degree, but they managed to follow my directions, and we made our way out to the main hall of the nightclub.

A small crowd had gathered around the other bouncer I'd hit on the way in. He was only now pulling himself up off the floor where I'd left him. Without any attempt to change my speed, I punched him in the face as we went by. It was very gratifying. He went back down, unconscious, and the crowd moved back to make room for the girls and me to get by.

I led the young women along the side of the large room opposite where Demi sat, hoping to avoid her notice. When we got to the front exit, the bouncers there stared at our little blanket-wrapped group in astonishment and made room for us to get through the crowd of clubgoers waiting to get in.

I was about to start herding the girls toward my truck when I noticed a small group of men standing across the street watching the entrance to the club. In the centre of the group, standing with his muscular arms folded in a power pose was Daniel. We crossed over to them.

"What are you doing here?" I asked

"We're here to help," Daniel said, a big smile on his face. "It looks like you didn't need us."

Three of Daniels group, all of them tough-looking tattooed guys, were putting their arms around the young girls with surprising gentleness. One man, whose acne scarred face I would have found threatening in the past, was removing his jacket and putting it around one of the shivering girls. He then picked her up to get her off the cool concrete.

Standing next to Daniel and glaring at me with his perpetually menacing expression was my friend, the doorman from Rebellion House. I smiled at him. His face darkened, his glare intensifying. He might have also grown a bit taller.

I peeled the drugged little girl off my chest and handed her to Daniel.

"Can you see that she gets home? I have someone waiting for me."

Daniel took the blanket-wrapped girl in his arms.

"We'll take the other girls to their families. Is there anything to clean up inside?"

"There are some people in a room in the back that somebody should do something about. I don't think you'll have much trouble getting in. But wait 'till I leave with my date if you don't mind."

I didn't know what Daniel and his guys would do with the creeps in the club, and I didn't care. I considered calling Corporal Tkatchuk and decided against it. If I did, I'd be sicking the cops on Daniel's guys as much as on the creeps in the back room. I looked at my watch and was surprised to see that it was already almost one in the morning. Time flies when you're having fun!

Demi was coldly quiet all the way home. I guess she didn't buy my excuse that I'd had bathroom issues. The truck didn't quite tip over when she slammed the door without saying good-night.

I was surprised to find my apartment door slightly ajar when I got home. Entering, I was even more surprised to find my friend, the Rebellion Doorman, sitting in my favourite spot on the couch. He got up when he saw me.

"She is asleep in her room. She will be fine," He said. His

voice had a gravelly, whispery quality to it like the tattoo artist had gotten a little too aggressive when working on his Adam's apple.

"Thanks," I replied as he headed to the door. I smiled at him. I'm sure he would have smiled back if he knew how.

I went down the hall and peeked in at the sleeping girl. She was completely hidden under her covers. 'She' was completely hidden under the covers. I shook my head. We had a lot to talk about.

I closed her door and headed to my room. I'm pretty sure I was asleep before I got there.

CHAPTER FIFTEEN

I was enjoying a coffee on the balcony when Aaron got up the next morning. I soon heard the water running in the bathroom in preparation for one of 'her' long baths. So many things actually made perfect sense in retrospect. When she emerged a while later, she was dressed as a girl. For the first time she poured herself a coffee, and when she came out to the balcony, her movements seemed distinctly more feminine.

"How are you?" I asked.

"Fine." Her eyes flicked up to briefly meet mine, and there was a smile in them.

"Do you feel like talking?" I asked.

"Who...what are you?" Aaron asked back. She asked it calmly, not like the first time she asked, a few weeks earlier.

Then it had been a challenge. "And, were you really moving that fast, or was that the drugs?"

Mathew's words came back to me, and I decided it was time for honesty. I motioned for Aaron to follow and we went back inside the apartment. It wouldn't be good to have this conversation overheard by someone listening from a window or balcony.

"My name is Orville Olson," I said, pausing for dramatic effect, "And I'll be ninety-two years old next month."

Aaron looked up at me with an expression of wonder, her head slowly shaking back and forth.

"But before I tell you more, I want to know for sure that you are okay. What you went through the last couple of days, that had to have been pretty tough."

"I'm okay. Somehow, I knew you would come. And all they did was drug me and dress me up like a slut. I don't think anyone raped me. Besides, it's not the first time I've been through something like that."

"Your mother's friend?" I asked.

Aaron looked up at me and for a moment appeared to be on the verge of tears.

"Holy Fuck!" I said with quiet anger edging my voice. There was no excited reaction to my choice of words this time.

I had no words for her. I couldn't imagine what something like that must have been like.

"And you never told your mother?"

"She deserves to be happy. She's the best Mom in the world. She really is. She went through hell for me. She would do anything for me. I couldn't tell her. I couldn't take away her happiness."

"Is he good to her? Can you be sure?"

"She says he is. She seems good when we talk." Aaron looked down at her coffee and took a slow sip.

"I think I'd like to meet this 'friend' of your mother's

someday. Have a little chat with him."

Aaron looked up at me, her eyes twinkling, the sadness gone.

"Ninety-two freaking years old!" she practically shouted it.

"Yeah. It's kind of a long story. It started the day we met I guess."

We then began a question and answer session that went back and forth for over an hour. Aaron asked most of the questions, and I told her pretty much everything that happened since the morning of my accident. Every once and a while I would think of something to ask her.

I learned that she was actually eighteen years old and had always been a bit of a tomboy. She talked about all of the things her mother had done for her as she grew up. Things like fighting with the kid's hockey league to let her play with the boys. Like being her best friend when the other girls her age treated her the way kids do when someone is different.

"Matthew said that you were 'Two-Spirited'. I think his exact words were 'Uniquely two-spirited. Is that what he meant? That you were a tomboy?"

"I guess kind off," she said slowly. "He knows I'm a girl."

"I don't know how to ask this, so don't take me the wrong way, but, do you want to be a boy?"

"Wow! You really are ninety years old, aren't you?"

"Ninety-one. Well?"

"Hell no!" Aaron laughed loudly. "I love my body the way it is!"

I pictured her body as it had looked the night before. I could feel my face heating up.

"It's just safer on the street if you're a guy, you know. And it's like having a secret identity. Sometimes I like being a girl. Sometimes I like being a boy. When I'm dressed like a boy, I feel like a boy, I guess. But I'm me no matter how I'm dressed."

We were quiet for a bit.

"It all kind of makes sense now," Aaron said. "I mean, the way you talk. Even the things you think are funny."

"What is so wrong with the way I talk?" I was still a little sensitive about it, I guess.

"It's kind of the speed you talk as much as anything else. And the not swearing, and all the 'dangs' and 'derns'."

I did my best to roll my eyes.

"And some words you get completely wrong!" Aaron was on a roll now, speaking much faster than was her norm. "When you say 'tomorrow' it comes out 'tomorrel'. And the place where you and all the other millionaires love shopping? It's called 'Walmart' not 'Walmark'.

"Dammit," I said, quite deliberately. "I've been talking the same way for ninety years. It's not easy to change."

"I'm sorry for making fun of you. It really does seem to make sense now. But you never answered my question. Did you really move as fast as you seemed to move the other night? I mean they did shoot me up with something."

"Yeah, I guess I did. But, before we go there, you've got to promise to help me learn how to talk like someone who looks my age, or someone who is the age that I look. You know what I mean."

Aaron smiled, and she was very much a pretty young woman.

"The first time I knew it was happening was when Bouchard's guys tried to beat me up in the alley out back."

"WHAT?"

I told her everything that happened in the time we'd been apart.

"I was too busy to test it again until I got to the nightclub, but it worked again then. I think that I can somehow affect the flow of time. I kind of push with my mind and everything around me slows down. That's it, I guess. It's not really that

I'm moving fast, but everything else is moving slow."

"That is totally fucking mind-blowing! Sorry."

"You should try it from in here," I said, pointing to my head.

"Do it now!" Aaron said excitedly.

I gave a mental push and then got up from the couch and moved quickly to the dining room table and sat down. I then did the mental relaxing thing, it was like letting out a slow breath but inside my head, and time returned to normal. I was happy to find that there was no accompanying headache. I had been concerned that that might be part of the deal, but the pain I felt at the nightclub must have been the temporary result of the blow I'd received.

"Holy fucking shit that's cool! Sorry!"

I ignored her language.

"What did it look like to you?" I asked.

"It was like you were a blur. But it's like you didn't make any sound. Like, no sound at all. Like you were in a vacuum, kind of."

Again, I pushed at time, and as I moved back to the couch, I said, "What does it sound like this time." Then I relaxed out of it.

"What did it sound like that time?" I asked.

"Same thing. No sound at all. How long can you do it?"

"I don't know. I haven't really tested it."

"Why don't we go out into the country where nobody can see us and see what you can do."

"Why don't we go and get some breakfast first. Maybe I'll see If I can use my power to eat as fast as you."

We drove up river to an area called Cranberry Flats. It's a popular summer hangout for sun-worshipers, but it was a little late in the year for tanning, and we were the only visitors. The large, sandy beaches were an excellent place to test this strange new ability.

Giving the mental push, I jogged down the beach and then relaxed back to normal speed. Pushing again, I walked back to Aaron. She perceived no difference in my speed. In both cases, I was a blur. I pushed again and walked around her clapping my hands and shouting. Aaron again reported that I made no sound at all.

It reinforced my suspicion that I was somehow moving myself physically outside of the normal flow of time. It made sense to me that any sound I made when outside of time would be created at a frequency different from normal sound. I resolved to do some reading about sound frequencies and time. This was raising questions in my mind that just never came up in my previous life.

Then I noticed something odd. The places I walked or ran when I was outside of the normal time flow showed footprints in the sand that were considerably shallower than those I made in regular time. I pushed again and ran down the beach, paying particular attention to the sensation of my feet hitting the earth. Sure enough, the sand felt much more solid underfoot when 'out of time'.

"I want to try something else," I said, as I walked a short distance away from Aaron. "Throw a rock at me."

Aaron picked up a rock and threw it in my direction. I pushed. The rock slowed down to where it was hard to distinguish its movement. I walked over to stand next to where the stone was passing, and its movement became more apparent. I reached out to grab the rock out of the air, and when it came in contact with the palm of my hand, there was a sharp pain where it touched and then a kind of pushing feeling as I slowed the rocks progress. But that pushing feeling lasted only a split second in time as I was experiencing it. I threw the rock upward, expecting it to slow shortly after leaving my hand. Instead, it continued upward at the speed I had tossed it and went many times higher than my effort would seem to have justified. I relaxed back to normal time and watched the rock go up and then fall back down, landing in the river several feet away.

"Holy Cow!" I exclaimed.

"That was so crazy!" Aaron exclaimed at the same time. "I can see you moving, 'cause I kind of knew what you were going to do, or at least where you were going to go, but you really are just a blur. Where did the rock go?"

I told her what I experienced and then picked up another rock, pushed again, and then threw it as hard as I could, relaxing back afterward. The stone abruptly vanished in the distance. Good thing I had chosen to throw upstream and away from the city because I have no idea where that rock landed. My guess is it was several miles away. I hope it didn't hit anyone.

"I heard that," Aaron said.

"What did you hear?"

"It was kind of a popping sound."

"That makes a kind of sense. If I am moving out of time, it stands to reason that anything I am holding moves out of time with me. It explains why I don't leave my clothes behind."

"Too bad," Aaron interjected.

That flustered me a bit, another reminder that she was a girl and not the young boy I had believed her to be. I stood for a moment with my mouth hanging open. Girls are considerably more forward today than they had been in my youth.

"Sorry," she said. "But not really."

"Anyway, when I threw the rock it re-entered the regular timestream and, when it did, it retained the momentum I had given it when outside of the time stream, so when it re-entered, it created a kind of mini sonic boom."

We had begun walking southward along the riverbank, and as we rounded a bend in the river, we spotted some Canada Geese as they waddled along the shore. They noticed us at the same time and took flight. I grabbed Aaron, picking her up and pushing with my mind at the same time. Sure enough, the world slowed down around the two of us.

Walking briskly, we approached the slow flying geese. We were able to catch up to the geese with ease and were both astounded to see them slowly flapping their wings as we walked next to them. We got so close to one that Aaron reached out to touch its wing but pulled back at the last instant.

"We're freaking them out," she said excitedly.

I relaxed us back into normal time. The geese flew away, honking noisily.

"Obviously sound travels between us when we are both moving outside of time. I heard what you said," I said.

"You really are some kind of nerd, aren't you? We just experienced something no one has ever experienced before, and you're like analyzing the science."

"Bookworm," I replied, but when she looked back at me quizzically, I said, "Never mind."

We turned and started walking back toward where we had parked, and I noticed again the shallower than natural footprints I had made in the sand. It brought to mind a comic book superhero who could move so fast he was able to run on water.

"Wait here," I said and pushed as I began to run along the water's edge. Running as fast as I could, I veered into the slow flowing river. The result was not what I had hoped for. The water did resist my feet slightly more than would be normal, but it was far from running on a hard surface. Instead, my feet sunk into what felt like thick mud. As you might imagine, running in thick mud does not go well. I tumbled, slapping the water with my face and upper body and phasing back into time from the shock. It was far from pleasant. It felt like being slapped by a giant cold, wet hand. Hard.

"Oh my God! What did you do?" Aaron asked, laughing.

I picked myself up out of the cold water. I let her laugh and instead of responding, pulled off my shirt and wrung it out. I began to shiver.

"Let's go home," Aaron said. "I'll let you barbecue steaks for dinner.

So, we did. And I did.

Aaron surprised me by coming out to dinner still dressed as a girl. A very pretty young girl. She knew how to do her makeup. It was artfully and subtly applied to accent her already large eyes. Who knew? She wore snug jeans and a white shirt, a feminine version of a man's dress shirt. The look was pretty classy and again reminded me of a young Audrey Hepburn.

She was quiet while we ate, responding to the questions I asked with more than the one word answers I was accustomed to getting from the 'boy' Aaron, but adding little more to the conversation. She ate slower than usual, another contrast to the young roommate I'd come to know. I wondered if she, herself, was conscious of the differences.

When we finished eating, she set her cutlery down and placed her hands on the table palms down like she was bracing herself. She spoke without looking up at me.

"Max, now that you know I'm a girl, is it okay if I still live with you?"

That one stunned me! No wonder she was so quiet during the meal.

"Of course! I would miss you if you weren't here!"

Aaron jumped up, came around the table, gave me a hug and a big kiss on the cheek and then ran off to her room.

I couldn't get the silly grin off my face as I cleaned up the dishes.

Elsie, I think I'm going to like having a girl around.

CHAPTER SIXTEEN

The next morning Aaron, the boy, and I went to see Matthew. As I placed a Caramel Macchiato between Matthew and his laptops he looked up.

"Orville, Aaron."

"Good morning, Matthew," I said.

"You okay?" Matthew asked, looking at Aaron.

"Good," Aaron replied.

"We are in your debt," Matthew said to me.

"No debt," I said. "I could use your advice as to what to do next. There is still a monster on the loose."

"More than one, I would say. Daniel and his boys found only empty rooms in the back of that club. However, you saved three young women, for which we are very grateful. But girls have gone missing before them, and I fear that many more will be taken if we don't stop Bouchard and whoever he is working with."

"Damn," I said.

Matthew and Aaron looked briefly at each other. Aaron smiled, and I noticed something close to a twinkle in Matthew's eyes.

Aaron said, "I know, hey?"

I said, "Yeah, yeah. Orville cursed," which got me a giggle from Aaron.

"I don't believe we have anything that Corporal Tkatchuk can make use of," Matthew said. "I wouldn't think he could even get a warrant to search the club, based on our story alone."

"Nonetheless, I intend to go and talk to him this morning. He needs to know what I found there. There were other creeps in that room with those girls, and a woman was making a video recording. They have to be stopped, and I don't think they're going to stop just because I beat up on a couple of bouncers."

"Agreed. We need to put pressure on Bouchard. He is the only guy we've got at this point," Matthew said. "I suspect that Bouchard is now concerned about what is known about him. You have shown up out of nowhere, confronted him in front of others and then broken up one of his parties. If I were Bouchard, I would be wondering who you are, what you know, and how you know what you know. I believe this does give you an advantage."

"I have an appointment to see him at his office tomorrow afternoon. I'll ask him what he does in his spare time."

It turns out, Matthew's smile is as big as his brothers when he decides to use it.

"Daniel would like you to stop by and see him. Aaron, can you stay? I need you."

When I pulled up in front of Rebellion House, my friend the doorman was sitting on the front step, smoking a cigarette. He stood up as I approached and stood to the side as I went in. Yes, I smiled. And no, he didn't. I spun back on him and extended my hand.

"My name's Max. I never caught yours."

"Gabriel," he growled at me.

"Good to know you, Gabe. Thanks again…"

"Gabriel," he growled a little louder.

"Gabriel," I corrected. "Thanks for taking care of my friend." I turned and headed upstairs. *Well, that went well,* I thought.

Daniel's smile was characteristically bright and cheery as he got up from behind his desk. He was wearing shorts and a t-shirt and was covered in sweat, which accented his muscles and made him look like he was carved out of rock. We shook hands.

"I don't think Gabriel likes me very much."

"Really? Why do you say that?"

I tried to look incredulous. He laughed. This time, I was okay with it and grinned back.

"You did good, Max. We owe you!"

"I'm not done. So, they were gone when you got in there, I hear."

"We found their orgy-room but nothing else. We didn't want to stick around to do a thorough search. Someone was bound to let the police know that 'Rebellion' beat up on some bouncers."

"I thought you might be blamed for that. There were three guys in there and a woman making a video. I didn't recognize any of them. I'm going to talk to Bouchard tomorrow. I think I'll ask him who they were." As I was saying this my cell phone chirped in my pocket. I pulled it out. "I got a text message!" I said with a little too much enthusiasm. "New," I said, holding up the phone.

"Congratulations," Daniel said, smirking and shaking his head slightly. "I just wanted to say thank you for what you've done. Do you want backup when you see Bouchard?"

"I'll be fine," I said. "I'll keep you informed."

When I got back out to the truck, I managed to open up my messaging app. It was from Demi.

'Rumour has it something strange went down at WonderWall the other night. You had something to do with it, didn't you?'

'Yes. Sorry.' *Look at me! I'm texting like a twelve-year-old!*

I sat and waited for her response. I could feel Gabriel melting the side of my truck with his hate-ray vision. I avoided looking at him.

'I'm still pissed, but we should talk.'

'OK'

'I'm working today. C U later?'

'C U later.'

Turns out my dumb-ass grin was an effective shield against Gabriel's hate-ray.

'I'd like to speak with you.' This I sent to Detective Corporal Tkatchuk. *I am a technological genius!*

'Meet me at Cactus Club at 12. You can buy me lunch.'

'C U there.'

I described the events of two nights earlier to young Tkatchuk, leaving out the part about me slowing time. I also neglected to mention that Rebellion went in to do clean up.

"I heard rumours. Though you might have been involved. Why didn't you call me?"

"It was late," I said. I wanted to say something like, 'I didn't think someone your age should be up that late,' but managed to control myself.

"What happened to those young women?"

Of course, you'd have to ask that!

"Daniel Bird took them back to their families."

"You gave them to a gang!"

I had to admit that a few days ago that would've been my reaction.

"They've been through hell. They are likely in need of counselling. You really should have called me," The detective scolded.

"Call me old fashioned, but I believe what those girls needed was family. But you are right, I should have called you."

"At the very least, I could have checked out this 'Sex Room'. Maybe taken some pictures. I could have claimed I was in the club at the time. To do it now I'd need a warrant, and you haven't given me enough to get one. No idea who the men were?"

"No. Sorry. I'm not good with descriptions, either. Especially of half-naked men," I said. Then as an afterthought, "One of them has a sore shoulder if that helps."

"Really?" Tkatchuk's face had a squinting, skeptical expression.

"I kicked one of them in the shoulder. Hard."

The young man across from me looked like he had been kicked hard himself.

"Right shoulder?" he asked, slowly.

I nodded.

The detective's response was slow and quiet. "The Chief's been wearing a sling on his right arm the last two days."

I was shocked and intrigued.

"I think I'm going to go talk with your Chief this afternoon," I said.

"I think I'm going to be somewhere else," Tkatchuk said.

"I'd like to speak with the Chief."

"Do you have an appointment?" It wasn't cute the way the cop behind the counter said it.

"No, but he said he wanted to speak with me. Tell him I'm the guy he met two nights ago when he hurt his shoulder."

"Got a name?"

The cop at the counter looked skeptical but went back to a desk behind him and picked up a phone. After a short exchange, he hung up, sat down at the desk and stared at me. His phone rang, and there was another brief exchange and, hanging up, he buzzed me in.

I followed him to an elevator where he said, "Fourth floor, straight ahead."

Fourth floor straight ahead brought me to a reception room where a young uniformed cop sat at a desk. I told him who I was, and he indicated a row of chairs against a wall and told me the Chief would be with me shortly.

He kept me waiting there for about ten minutes. I wasn't surprised. He obviously knew who I was and what I wanted to talk with him about, so was spending some time either preparing his story or clearing his calendar. I waited patiently until the cop at the desk answered his phone and then got up and ushered me into the adjoining office.

Brian Vanderholt, Chief of Police, Saskatoon Police Services, was the man I'd kicked the night before last. Of course, I knew that. Were he not, I wouldn't have made it past the front desk. He watched me walk in and sit in a chair at his desk. My first impression was that he'd be a great poker player but revised that upon taking a deeper look into his eyes. He was afraid.

"Mr. Campbell. I need you to know that things are not the way they must seem to you."

"That's good because, to me, you *seem* to be a very ugly man." It's amazing how knowing you're in the right can give you courage. Well, knowing you're right *and* being able to mess with time can give you courage.

Vanderholt looked down at his hands and then back up into my eyes.

"I'm a good man and a good cop," he said. "At least I was until I met Henry Bouchard."

I didn't reply.

"Bouchard is a very evil man. I met him a few months ago, and he invited me to a party. He was already a big shot in town, so I thought I should accept his invitation. My wife was at her sister's in Calgary, so I went alone.

"Bouchard was a big talker right from the start, telling people that he was a very important man in Saskatoon and that gave him special privileges. He actually stood there and said that he could do things that other people couldn't. There was a small group of guests standing around him at the time, but I got the distinct impression that he was directing his comments at me.

"I've never been a big drinker, but I'll have one or two in social situations. I had just started sipping on my second drink when I noticed that I was feeling very warm. The rest of the night is a blur. The son of a bitch had something put in my drink. I don't even remember how I got home.

"The next morning, I was woken up by the doorbell, and one of my own cops was standing there with my keys and my car was in the driveway. He said to me, 'You sure enjoyed yourself last night, Chief!' I just took the keys and said, 'I'll see you at work.'

"After he left, I turned on my laptop to check my mail."

Vanderholt paused and looked at me like he didn't want to go on. I said nothing.

"Do I have to even tell you what I found? The fucker had pictures of me," Vanderholt was whispering now. Kind of a loud whisper, like he wanted to be shouting. "Pictures with women. I'm the fucking Chief of Police, and that bastard thinks he can blackmail me!"

"Can he?" I asked quietly.

He looked down at his hands again and slowly shook his head.

"I wanted to be a cop my whole life. When I was a kid I imagined I'd be catching the big criminals, the big gang bosses, or the genius cat-burglars that no one else could catch. I thought I'd catch the criminal masterminds. Fuck. What a joke. Do you know what cops do for a living? Do you know what we deal with every day? We deal with hot-tempered assholes that beat up their wives. We deal with small-time gangs that sell shit to school kids. We deal with crooks so stupid they practically beg to get caught. And these days we get to deal with the fucking creeps on the internet. The only smart people in the criminal game are the lawyers. There were never any criminal masterminds, and nothing I did ever really made a difference. So, I just did as well as I could, and I climbed the fucking ladder.

"And now, after thirty years, along comes a bonafide fucking criminal mastermind, and before I even know he's a bad guy he's fucked me up so bad all I can do is sit and watch."

"There has to be something you can do. Aren't there policies or methods? Surely this kind of thing has happened before."

"Sure, it's happened before. We have ways of dealing with blackmailers when people come to us. But, when it's us...when it's us it's a different story. The worst thing about it is he's inside my force. He's got cops working for him. Or maybe he's done the same thing to them, I don't know, but he knows he can work us against one another. I have friends in the RCMP that I would normally turn to, but their world is in fucking turmoil too. This shit is much bigger than just Henry Bouchard. I don't know where to turn."

The Chief was the perfect picture of the defeated man, once again staring at his hands and shaking his head.

"So, tell me about the other night."

"So, tell me who the fuck you are!" Vanderholt didn't quite yell it at me.

"Me? I'm just a guy who thinks that Bouchard has to be stopped. But he's not alone. He has friends. I'm just trying to determine if you're one of them. What about the other night?"

"The other day I called Bouchard. I told him that he wasn't going to get away with what he was doing. I told him I would resign. He fucking laughed at me. He said that we should talk, that he was sending someone to get me. Next thing you know two of my guys are in the outer office. My Fucking guys! They took me to see Bouchard at that fucking nightclub. Bouchard bragged again that he can do whatever he wants. Told me I was powerless. He bragged that selling girls was a bigger business than selling drugs and that he was making a killing. He said that no one cares if a few street girls go missing. Everyone just looks the other way. And then he told me that I was going to look the other way, too. That's what this is all about, you know. He doesn't just like young girls. He fucking sells them! And I don't know how, or where, or to who.

"When he was done bragging, my...his guys grabbed me, and someone injected me with something."

"Hmmm. I guess that explains the woman with the video camera. Bouchard must have felt that he needed a little more leverage on you. But you must have some cops you can trust."

"Sure. Most of my team are good cops. That's part of the problem. I don't want this fucker to get his claws into any more of my guys."

"Okay," I said. "I accept that you are another victim in this mess, and I wish I could help you. But I'm here to stop Bouchard before more girls go missing. Your problems are your problems. It might be that we can get enough evidence together that you can arrest him, and then you'll just have to deal with the fallout. I believe your story. Others will too. I can tell you that I've spoken with Detective Corporal Tkatchuk and I'm pretty sure that he's still one of the good guys. Talk to him.

Maybe the two of you can find a way to deal with your mess."

I turned a left.

The Colonial Bar and Grill was quiet when I got there. One old guy was sitting at the bar, and three tables were occupied. Demi was behind the bar.

"Cindy starts in ten minutes, and I can take a break," she said, coldly, as she handed me a Great Western Light. "Sit back there."

She had nodded toward a back corner of the bar, so, like any man with several decades of practice doing as he's told, I went and sat in the corner.

She's still pretty mad, I thought, as I watched her take drinks to one of the tables. *And she's still pretty!*

When Cindy arrived, she chatted with her for a few minutes and then walked over to me with two more beer. She set one in front of me and sat down. She took a drink of her beer and looked at me calmly for a moment. Without a smile on her face, her appearance was not completely devastating, just kind of stunning.

"I'm sorry…" I started to say, but Demi held up a hand.

"I just want to say something to you," she said calmly. "I am not some stupid little ditz, you know!"

I must have moved a facial muscle or something because her hand came back up and she continued.

"I'm not stupid, and I don't like being used. You could have been honest with me that our date was something other than a normal date. That way I wouldn't have made a fool of myself when all you wanted was an ulterior reason for being in that nightclub. I would have helped you, Max, because I liked you. If you had told me that you wanted to be some kind of hero, I could have helped you, and I might not have looked like such a fool."

She had gone through her entire little speech without

raising her voice and without accusing me of anything other than not being totally upfront with her.

'Elsie, did you coach this girl?'

"Demi, you are absolutely justified in being mad at me. I was unfair to you, and I used you, and I'm not even sure why I did it. All I can tell you is that I'm new at this stuff. The dating stuff *and* the hero stuff."

When Demi started to respond, I did the hand thing back at her. I'm not totally spineless.

"I guess I wanted to ask you out and I used the need to go to that nightclub to give me the courage to do it. I know that's pathetic, and it was wrong, and I'm sorry. I am very flattered. I'm sorry that you feel you made a fool of yourself, but I don't think you did. I may have been devious, but I did want to ask you out, and I'm am still quite proud to have gone out on a date with the prettiest girl I've ever met."

"Oh, my God! You were doing so good, but 'Prettiest girl I've ever met'? *That* was pathetic!" Demi said, rolling her eyes. But she smiled at the same time.

"Yep. That's me. Pathetic. No argument. I am really sorry, Demi!"

"Well…"

"I'd really like another chance. A real first date some time."

"Well, we'll see. So, what happened the other night?" Demi asked, changing the subject. "Rumour has it you broke up some really creepy shit going on down there."

"Can I tell you another time? There's still stuff I have to take care of, and I'd prefer it was over before we talk about it, or before we have our first date."

"You are a very strange man, Max. But I think you're a good man. And besides, you are very fun to look at." She gave me a smile. It took considerable effort to keep my feet from doing a little happy dance under the table.

"It's good we can both enjoy ourselves," I said, smiling

back at her.

CHAPTER SEVENTEEN

There was much more activity around Bouchard's office than the first time I visited. Six vehicles sat in the parking lot, a couple of guys in hard hats were working on the roof, and when I walked inside, I found the pretty receptionist showing a young couple some brochures at her desk.

"Ah, Monsieur Campbell, you are here for your appointment with Monsieur Bouchard."

Could she know what an absolute bastard her boss was? I decided that she couldn't possibly know, based primarily on the way she said 'appointment'.

She got up and opened the door behind her desk and said, "Follow me."

I followed her down a short hall and past an open doorway.

"Hey, Max! How you doing?" a voice called from the room as I passed. Looking in I found the salesman, Brad, sitting at a desk across from an older couple.

"Hey, Brad." It was all I had time to say. I didn't want to fall too far behind the receptionist and lose my way.

At the end of the hallway, she opened another door and leaning in said, "Monsieur Campbell," and then stepped out of the way to let me pass. She closed the door behind me.

The room was large. The furniture was large. Made me wonder if something was small. Henry Bouchard sat behind a large desk, and behind him, the two men who had accosted me behind my apartment stood like big, ugly gargoyles.

"Hi, guys!" I said to the gargoyles. They just glared at me doing their best to look menacing. My friend Gabriel could have taught these guys a thing or two.

"Bouchard," I said, sitting down.

"Mister Campbell! I've been looking forward to seeing you again." The creepy bastard seemed to genuinely mean what he was saying. A chill went down my spine.

"I've been looking forward to seeing you as well, Bouchard, so that I could tell you what a sick goddamn bastard you are." This appeared to ruffle the gargoyles' feathers but had no effect on their boss. "I wanted to tell you that I'm shutting down your little side business."

"Really, Mr. Campbell!" Bouchard smiled and looked surprised. "What side business is that?"

"Let's not play games, Bouchard." This was starting to sound like a bad detective novel. "You've been kidnapping girls and selling them. But only after you have your own sick way with them."

"Well, Mr. Campbell," Bouchard chuckled. "I am a businessman selling a product. What kind of businessman would I be if I didn't do a little 'Quality Control'?"

"Like I said, I'm shutting you down."

"Mr. Campbell!" His repeated use of my last name was starting to seem very condescending. "You are a very interesting man. When we first met, you somehow had knowledge that you should not have had. And then, when Micky and Michael here told me they were unable to make an impression on you, I must say I was quite surprised."

Despite the tension I was feeling, I almost laughed when he named the gargoyles. It didn't help that he gave Michael the French pronunciation making it sound, to my ears, like a woman's name.

"And then, Mr. Campbell, you show up at my club, and you interfere with some business that I was conducting there. So, I did a little research into you, and do you know what I found, Mr. Campbell? Nothing. You seemed to have come out of nowhere. It is as if you didn't even exist until a couple of months ago. That is very interesting, Mr. Campbell. Very interesting indeed."

I'd had enough. I stood up, causing the gargoyles to tense a bit.

"I don't give a shit what you find 'interesting', Mr. Bouchard." My attempt to mimic his condescension failed miserably. "I am not going to let your little business continue in this city!"

"What is it you think you are going to do to stop me, Mr. Campbell?"

Before I had a chance to reply, he reached out to a computer monitor sitting on his desk and turned it toward me. On it, a video was playing. It looked like security footage taken in a dimly lit room full of couches and beds. As my eyes were drawn to it, almost against my will, a man in the video moved so quickly across the room he was little more than a blur as he struck two men knocking them to the floor.

"Like I said, Mr. Campbell. Very interesting."

"If you think this video is some kind of threat, Bouchard, you are mistaken. Show it to whoever you like. No one will believe it. These days a ten-year-old kid could create a video like that on his phone."

"You misunderstand, Mr. Campbell. I simply wish to impress upon you why I believe you will be a very special member of my organization. I man with your gifts can do things for me that no one else could do. Isn't that right, Mr. Campbell?"

If he says 'Mr. Campbell' one more time I might kill him and then go ask Matthew for new ID with a different name.

"You see, Mr. Campbell, you will work for me for the same reason that many other people work for me. People like Chief Vanderholt, for example. You will work for me because you have people you care about. You do have people you care about, don't you Mr. Cam…"

With a mental push, I threw myself out of my chair, and before the gargoyles could even move, I'd punched both of them in the face. It felt like punching concrete, and each of their faces distorted in a way that faces shouldn't distort. I let normal time resume before turning on Bouchard. I wanted him aware of what I was going to do to him.

"Amazing!" Bouchard said like he was giving me his approval. He pushed a button on his desk phone and said, "Show in my next appointment, Louise."

I looked back at the gargoyles slumped against the wall. Each looked like he'd been bashed in the face with a baseball bat. And yet, here was Bouchard, having someone else ushered into his office like it was nothing out of the ordinary. I couldn't believe it.

"I'm sorry Mr. Campbell, but our time is up." He was acting as if things like this happened every day in his world. I was flabbergasted. Already, I could hear someone coming down the hall. He got up and stepped around in front of his desk and held his arm out toward his door. "We will speak again soon," he said.

I was so stunned that I followed his outstretched arm and

stepped toward the door.

"Oh, and thank you for buying my penthouse, Mr. Campbell," Bouchard said as the door opened, and two men stepped in. At the same moment, Bouchard placed his hand on my shoulder.

***

Suddenly, I was sitting on the edge of a bed in a sunlit bedroom. Laying on their sides and facing away from me were two naked young women, covered to their waists with a thin white sheet. They appeared to be asleep.

My heart beat strongly as I looked at the girls. Feelings of power and pride filled my chest, and I smiled to myself. Under these feelings, a hunger burned. I wanted to devour these delicate creatures.

I reached out and caressed the arm of the closest sleeping girl. My hand moved up her arm, over her shoulder and down onto her back where my finger traced the shape of an unusual dragonfly tattoo on the girl's shoulder blade. I began to unbutton my shirt.

***

A door closed behind me, and I found myself in the short hallway outside of Bouchard's office. Louise, the young receptionist, was gazing at me with a look of puzzled concern.

"Are you okay, Monsieur Campbell?"

"Uh, yeah. Yeah." I wasn't.

Louise led me down the hallway, into the outer office and held the exit door open for me as I trudged like an automaton out to the street. Momentum must have taken me to my truck because my brain certainly wasn't directing the process. It was waffling back and forth between thoughts of the forward flash, and the unbelievable gall Bouchard exhibited in his office.

As panic and disbelief came close to overwhelming me, I leaned against the front of my truck and closed my eyes. As I did so the vision of the flash filled my mind.

The memory came to sharper focus as I visualized the tattoo on the young woman's naked back. The image of the dragonfly was created by matching the colour of the ink to several small birthmarks. The artist had used the birthmarks as part of his creation to produce an artful piece of work that was both subtle and beautiful.

The panic intensified and very nearly overwhelmed me. The world turned grey and almost went black. I would have fallen to the ground had I not been leaning on my truck for support. I took several deep breaths and fumbled my way into the driver's seat.

Jesus, Max, get a grip! I told myself. *This is not the time to fall apart!*

As I drove slowly away, I shook my head in an unsuccessful attempt to clear the image of my great-granddaughter's tattoo from my mind.

PART THREE

CHAPTER EIGHTEEN

The University of Saskatchewan Human Resources Offices are located in the Administration Building and adjoining MacKinnon Building. I had been there once before, to see my great-granddaughter's office, but my recollection of the visit was shaded by the physical challenge of getting there, almost obscuring my memory of the directions I had been following. It was a heck of a long haul for a ninety-year-old man. I was pretty sure that I could find her again, provided she was still in the same office, but I needed a plausible reason for being there, so I swung by the University Services Building on my way and made note of a name from an office door.

I was going to see Jenny, after having spent the better part of two hours making sure I was not being followed. I was also allowing myself time to calm down after the shock I had received at Bouchard's office.

I had decided weeks earlier that I would avoid any contact with the members of my former family. They would have moved on with their lives after the passing of their patriarch and, as Max Campbell, I had nothing to offer any of them.

Then, the most recent future flash with Henry Bouchard had revealed that my favourite great-granddaughter would, somehow, end up in his clutches. It was inconceivable. How could Bouchard have made a connection between me and my former life? Could it simply be a coincidence? It seemed unlikely considering Bouchard's "people you care about" comment. Somehow, Bouchard had found out who I really was and was going to use my loved-one to control me.

The only other possible explanation was that the girl in the flash wasn't Jenny. Was it possible that another girl who looked very similar to my great-granddaughter would have an identical tattoo in the same location on her back? The artist had designed the tattoo to incorporate birthmarks that were on Jenny's shoulder blade. But he could have been so proud of his work that he recreated for another customer. Possible, I suppose, but not likely. No, I had to accept that, somehow, Bouchard knew who I was.

It took a while, but I finally realized that the connection between me and Jenny had to be me. Obviously, Bouchard would find out about her because, in my panic, I would lead him directly to her. Yes, that had to be it. And, it was a situation I could control. If I simply kept to my original resolve and avoided ever making contact with Jenny, Bouchard would never learn about her.

I began to calm down. For a short time I believed that I had solved the problem and my panic subsided. But, gradually, it was replaced with an insuperable dread. I had never known a flash forward to be inaccurate. In every flash I had ever followed up on, the vision I had received was an exact preview of what was to come. I was forced to accept that, no matter what steps I took, the future I had witnessed in Henry

---

Bouchard's office was going to take place. I could only act to affect the aftermath. To do that, I would have to get in touch with my great-granddaughter.

Nonetheless, I did what I could to avoid leading Bouchard directly to her. I spent a couple of hours driving around the city, making last-minute lane changes and turns, and parking in places where anyone following would have to make themselves visible in order to keep me in sight. I felt fairly confident that no one could possibly have tracked me to the University.

I parked in a small parking lot north of The Administration Building and plugged the meter. Entering through a side entrance, I made my way to the front of the building and bounded up the stairs to the third-floor landing. Through a door at the top of the stairs, and seated behind a desk was my great-granddaughter, Jenny. I took a deep breath and walked in.

Jenny looked up and smiled, and I was reminded that she was my best-looking offspring.

"Hi," I said, smiling back. "I'm looking for Connie Sanders." It was the name from the office door in the University Services Building. I had recalled Jenny complaining that too much of her time was spent redirecting people to Human Resources Staff officed in other buildings, the result of her desk's proximity to the elevators and stairs, and the administration's decision to locate Human Resources staff in every possible building on campus.

"Sorry, but you have the wrong building," Jenny responded, not losing her smile.

"Oh! I was told she was with Human resources."

"Yeah, she is, but her office is actually in the Maintenance Building. Don't ask why. The answer won't make any sense." Jenny's demeanour was chipper throughout the exchange, masking the frustration I knew she was experiencing.

"Hey, no worries! I can use the exercise, just point me in the right direction," I said.

Jenny quite deliberately looked me up and down and responded, "You, definitely, do not need exercise!"

She was flirting with me. I was flattered and creeped out at the same time. But, hey, she had no idea that the young man in front of her was actually her late great-grandfather. And, even though I most definitely did know, my young male body was reacting to her flirtatiousness. My heart rate increased, and I started to perspire.

'I'm sorry, Elsie. I'm turning into some kind of sex maniac or something!'

'I always thought you were, Old Goat!'

"Uh, thanks," I responded. "Where's the Maintenance Building?"

"It's actually called the University Services Building, and if you're walking, the easiest way is to go through the Ag Building then go left. It's on maintenance road. You can't miss it."

I stood looking at her for a minute. Jenny had always been a cute kid. Truth be told she was now actually very pretty. Her style, I'd recently learned, was known as 'Goth', choosing dark clothes and makeup shades, and keeping her hair dark with the occasional streak of bold colour as an accent. Her choices were perfect for someone with her large dark eyes and light complexion.

My contemplation of her had just passed the comfort point. She gave me a quizzical look and seemed about to ask if there was anything else when I remembered I didn't really have to find the University Services Building. I had other reasons for being there.

"Oh, uh, sorry! It's just that you look familiar." It was the perfect recovery. "Have we met before?"

"Yeah, weird," Jenny responded. "I was thinking the same thing. I'm sure I would have remembered you, though." Again with the up and down scan of my body. She was so blatantly flirting.

"Ha, uh, thanks!" To say this situation was awkward for me

would be understating it. I liked the flirting but at the same time kept reminding myself that this was my great-granddaughter. It brought to mind the cartoon with the little devil on one shoulder and an angel on the other. "My name's Max," I said, extending a hand.

"Jenny," she responded, reaching out to shake, and...

Nothing. I was so expecting a flash of panic, fear and revulsion that, when I received nothing, it left me standing there shaking her hand long after the comfort threshold had passed. I pulled my hand away like hers had bitten me.

Jenny just smiled like she was mildly amused and reached for a business card from a holder on her desk. She wrote quickly on the back and handed it to me.

"That's my cell number," she said. "Call me sometime. We could figure out how we know each other. Maybe over drinks."

By this time, I was so flustered and embarrassed that it was important I make a confident, gentlemanly exit.

"I will, Jenny, and thanks," I said, nodding my head slightly, and as I spun around to leave I walked right into the metal doorframe. I'm sure the resulting, resonant 'BONG' could be heard for blocks.

Well, I thought, as I hopped into my truck and rubbed my sore forehead, *that, in so many ways, went both better and worse than it could have.*

I had hoped to find a way to keep in touch with Jenny, and she'd provided me with a reason to stay in touch. Unfortunately, her suggestion that I give her a call was obviously motivated by a romantic interest. Of course, that made me extremely uncomfortable.

I had wanted to shake hands with her, and in doing so corroborate the flash I'd received from Bouchard. We shook hands. I got nothing. That could mean one of two possibilities, as far as I could determine. Either the girl in Bouchard's bed wasn't Jenny, an option which was fine by me, but would not change the fact that I needed to put a stop to Bouchard's activities, or it was Jenny, and being in his bed was not traumatic enough to bring about a future flash. I supposed there were ways that might be understandable. She could be drugged, a technique Bouchard and his people have used before. Or maybe she ends up in that bed with another girl but is somehow unaware she's about to be accosted by a middle-aged pervert. But then for it not to become traumatic, thereby resulting in a future flash, she would have to be rescued from the situation before that situation becomes traumatic. This was beginning to make my head hurt. Granted, that could be the doorframes fault.

'What do I do now, Elsie?'

"You'll think of something, Orville. You always do.'

That's the problem with asking ghosts in your imagination for help. They never actually provide you with ideas you haven't already come up with.

There was something else about the encounter that was troubling me, and I was having a hard time nailing down what it was. The young woman I'd just met looked like my great-granddaughter, she had the same voice and many of the mannerisms I remembered, and I had found her behind the desk in the office where I knew she worked. Yet it didn't seem that she was the Jenny I'd known and loved. Part of it, I knew, was that I remembered a girl who was somewhat shy and reserved. She had been that way as a small child, and she had seemed that way when she visited me as an adult. This look-alike Jenny was anything but shy and reserved. She had greeted me with a big, bright smile and had even been so bold as to give me her cell number and suggest I give her a call. The nonagenarian in me found such a thing very forward for a young woman, but I had to admit that in this day and age it was probably not that unusual. So, it's not that I can say there is anything wrong with the way she acted or what she did, it's just that neither her actions nor her personality jived with what I'd expected of her.

But was this something that I should be bothered by? Did the way I felt about it have anything to do with the situation as it pertained to Bouchard and the missing young women? I was forced to admit it did not.

The reality is that people change a great deal when they move away from home and start lives of their own. I saw it in both of my children, and I recalled it from my own youth. But whenever a family gets together, the original dynamics remain, and people revert back to who they were when they still lived at home. My kids were both successful business people, and believe me, they could not be so if they acted in the real world the way they did whenever we all got together. Just because Jenny seemed shy and slightly awkward around her family didn't mean that she was that way when she was with other people or in different situations.

All of this is to say that I should not have been surprised to find that Jenny was not the same person in her world as she was whenever she shared my world. I should not have expected it. I had wanted her to be the same with the new me as she had been with her ancient great-grandfather and I was disappointed when I found her to be different.

A guy your age should know better, Orville, I told myself.

I pulled into my parking space behind my apartment and couldn't remember any part of the drive home. I wonder if I ran over anyone along the way.

"Chances are she was, will be, as drugged-up as they had me," Aaron said. "That might be why there wasn't enough emotion to cause a flash." Aaron had been pretty quick to adopt my terminology for my uncanny new abilities.

"Well, that would be a good thing," I replied. "I'd feel a lot better if I knew she'd not be traumatized by what she's going to go through."

"Or, she's not going to go through it at all, and there's some other explanation for your flash. Oh, and there's something else. You said that Bouchard touched you on your shoulder?"

We were sitting at the table in our small dining room. Aaron got up and went around behind me.

"What?" I asked.

"It just occurred to me that Bouchard may have put a GPS tracker on you, but I guess they haven't made one small enough yet. We should check your truck, though. He could have had his people put one on it."

"Damn!" I exclaimed. "I never even thought of that! Isn't that stuff just in movies and spy books."

"No, it's real," Aaron replied. "Matthew and I have used them a couple of times now."

"Really? We really need to talk more about what Matthew does for a living."

Aaron had explained a few weeks back that Matthew was some kind of technology and computer wizard who uses his skills to help people. One example she'd given me was when he managed to remove all copies of a compromising photo from the internet. A high school girl had sent a nude picture of herself to the wrong boy, like there's a right kind of boy to share a nude photo with, and he had posted it online. The girl's father paid Matthew a considerable sum to get it cleaned up. I would guess the service was well worth the price.

"You can buy trackers on Amazon for less than a hundred bucks," Aaron said.

"Damn."

"You're really getting good at that, Max," Aaron giggled.

I sneered at her.

"So, I probably led them right to Jenny."

"Not likely. A lot of people work at the University. They couldn't know who you visited unless you drove your truck right into her office."

"Good point." I felt a little better. "What am I going to do next? I don't think Bouchard will use his nightclub for any of his future parties. And I'm inclined to think that the girls weren't kept there the whole time."

"I was, but that was because they caught me snooping around at the club. It's all pretty fuzzy, but I think the other girls were just brought in the night you saved us."

"So, they've had another place where they keep the girls all along. How am I going to find it? I'm afraid I'm not much of a detective."

"Actually," said Aaron, "I have an idea."

CHAPTER NINETEEN

I set a Caramel Macchiato in front of Matthew.

"Orville," he said. "You don't have to buy me a coffee every time you visit, you know."

"That's coffee, is it? I'd wondered."

Matthew's eyes almost twinkled. He had the two laptops running in front of him as usual. He invited me to step to his side of the table and Aaron, who had been there with Matthew when I arrived, got up to make room for me. On one of the monitors was a map. Five small icons blinked on it. I sat down next to Matthew to take a closer look.

"Daniel had his boys put trackers on the vehicles parked around Bouchard's office. Since then Aaron and I have been learning a great deal about Bouchard and his men."

"Good plan!" I complimented Matthew.

"It was Aaron's idea," Matthew said.

Aaron, dressed as a boy, as usual, gave me an exaggerated smile.

"Three of the vehicles have visited the same location in the North Industrial Area," Matthew said. "Another vehicle has gone south of town toward Regina, but the signal has stopped on the highway and hasn't moved for over two hours. A fifth tracker has yet to leave the office."

"Did the tracker going south stop at an acreage or…" I was cut off by Matthew.

"No. I suspect that the tracker has fallen off of the vehicle. It never left the highway. Daniel is sending someone out to check right now."

"Then, maybe I should take a drive to the warehouse district," I said.

"Actually, Daniel just took some men there to take a look," Matthew said.

"You're not planning on keeping all of the fun to yourselves, are you?" I joked.

"This was our problem long before you got involved," Matthew said seriously. It was like he didn't want me to get too comfortable around him. "For now, we will wait."

I asked the two of them if they were hungry and was not surprised to get a 'yes' from Aaron. Matthew declined, so I went to the counter and got food for Aaron and me. If I keep eating at Starbucks I'm going to have to win another lottery soon.

I had just finished eating when Matthew got a call confirming that a badly beaten but still functioning tracker was found in a ditch south of the city. I asked Matthew if we knew which vehicle the tracker was on and, after he conferred with whoever was on the other end of the line, he told me it was a black Chevy Tahoe.

"Mickey and Michelle, the goons that Bouchard sent to rough me up, were driving a Tahoe," I said. "I wonder where they were headed. Can Daniel spare some guys to watch for that vehicle and put another tracker on it if it comes back to Bouchard's office?"

Matthew picked up another phone, he was still on the line with whoever he was talking to and typed out a message. I've never known anyone who multitasks quite like him. I wouldn't be surprised if he can type with his ears. He ended his phone conversation.

"Where did you learn to fight, Orville? Bouchard's men are tough bastards."

"I never really learned. I've got good reflexes, and I'm in pretty good shape. I worked hard on the farm."

Matthew made a small 'humph' sound. I noticed Aaron didn't look up during that brief interaction. It occurred to me that keeping my secrets might be putting a bit of a strain on the young girl. Mind you, she's proven herself to be pretty good with secrets.

Matthews phone buzzed again, and he answered. He had a brief conversation while typing on the laptop running the map program. He spoke quietly, and I could only make out a few of his words, but I could hear the other end of the conversation clearly. He was talking with his brother.

I was able to make out that Daniel and his men had visited a warehouse where the trackers had stopped but were unsuccessful in learning anything about what went on there. Most of the workers did have Quebecois accents, however, which pretty much proved their connection to Bouchard. They had to leave when Gabriel got in a fight with three of the men working there.

Matthew hung up the call and said, "Did you get that?"

"Most of it," I replied. "Is Gabriel okay?"

"No question. The three guys he was fighting aren't."

"Where did *he* learn to fight?" I asked.

"Gabriel was born fighting. Daniel left someone to watch the warehouse. He'll let us know if he learns anything."

"Can you call me if you hear anything? Sitting around is making me antsy. I think I'll see if our detective friend is busy. Aaron, do you need a ride home?"

"I'll hang here for a while and bus it home."

"Okay, but be careful. Bouchard threatened to hurt people I care about. Thanks again, Matthew."

"Orville," Matthew said.

Detective Tkatchuk responded to my text, and we met at the coffee shop down from the Cop Shop. He beat me to the punch and asked about my meeting with Bouchard before I had a chance to ask about the Chief.

"It was as if Bouchard arranged to have lots of people around the office when I stopped in," I told him. "Despite how tough his goons are, he must consider me something of a threat. He didn't act like it, though. He was in my face telling me that I might be useful to him. When I told him to go suck a rope, he responded by threatening me. Told me I had people I cared about."

"Fuck, he's a bold bastard! I talked to the Chief, and he told me about the mess Bouchard has him in. I can't believe the balls this guy has."

"Have the two of you come up with any ideas?"

"I hate to say it, but, no. Not yet. But we will. I think the Chief feels better with someone else knowing what's going on, even if it is only his token gay detective. He's not a bad man. He's just in a bad situation."

The young detective was watching my face when he made the 'gay' comment. I think he was trying to shock me, and he did. And I'm sure it showed. I decided we could talk about it another time and changed the subject, telling him about Matthew, Daniel and the trackers.

"All this is making me rethink my opinion of The Rebellion."

"Just 'Rebellion'. I don't get what the big deal is, but they're pretty sensitive about it."

"Fucking kooky, if you ask me. I had a chat with Detective Tremblay in Montreal. His situation with his superiors sounded so much like mine, I almost asked him if *he* was gay!"

This gay thing sure seemed important to him all of a sudden. I still didn't want to talk about it.

"I gotta think that Bouchard has way too many people by the nuts to be working alone," Tkatchuk said.

"I've been thinking the same thing, like, who is he selling to? Bouchard is likely just the tip of a very big iceberg. Possibly not even the tip. Nonetheless, if the Bird Brothers find a way to bring Bouchard down, we have to be prepared to do it, even if it means your Chief gets screwed in the process."

"If you and your Rebellion friends can get me anything to work with, I'll take it to a Crown Attorney. Vanderholt will just have to crawl his way out of whatever shit that lands him in."

"You need to watch your back," I told the young detective. "The chief didn't know if the cops on the force working for Bouchard are doing it because they want to, or because he has dirt on them. Either way, they could be dangerous."

"I watch my back with all of them. Always have."

Was it another reference to his sexual orientation or something else? It still seemed to me that young people were talking another language most of the time.

I was going to skip the rugby game that evening but decided sitting around worrying wasn't going to solve any of my problems. Before I headed to the game, I gave Jenny a call to see about arranging a date. She told me that I'd have to call back, as she was rushing off to her evening job. That was new.

I got to the pitch early, hoping to run a few practice plays with the guys before the game started. As it turned out, the teams playing before us were still on the field, so we watched the end of their game and critiqued their plays, which amounted to making fun of them and laughing a lot. We're a childish bunch of twits basically. As we watched, it clouded over and began to rain a little. Kyle was one of the last to show up, and as he walked toward us, I noticed he was limping a little.

"Oh, fuck, man! Not your back again!" one of the guys exclaimed. No one liked it when Kyle had to sit out a game.

"No, man, I'm good," He responded. As he got closer, it became apparent that he wasn't totally good. In addition to the limp, he was sporting a shiner on his left eye, and his bottom lip was swollen.

"Who'd you piss off, Mate?" Lucas asked.

Kyle didn't respond. Instead, he motioned me forward and, putting his arm over my shoulder began walking me away from the group. He wasn't leaning on me, but it felt like his arm weighed about a hundred and fifty pounds.

"I had a visit from some friends of yours when I got home from work," he said.

"Shit," I said.

"A couple of guys with French accents," he said.

"Shit," I said.

"Pretty tough guys. Managed to get the better of me. I almost had 'em at one point, though," he said.

"Damn," I said.

"Told me to give you a message. They said, 'Mr. Bouchard will be needing your help, soon.'"

"Son-f-a-bitch," I said.

Kyle smiled at me, but it must have hurt his wounded lip because it turned quickly into a grimace.

"Sorry, man!" I said. "I can't believe they'd go after you!"

"Who are they? What the hell have you gotten involved

in?"

"It's too long a story to tell right now," I said, noticing that the other teams were heading off the field. "Let's grab a beer after the game, and I'll fill you in."

"Beer good," Kyle said, deliberately sounding like the big dumb oaf he appeared to be.

We totally annihilated the other team. Kyle had some leftover aggression he needed to expend, and he shared it with every opponent he came in contact with. Basically, it was winning by intimidation. I am so glad I'm on his team.

Afterward, we begged off joining the rest of the team at Boston Pizza and went to The Colonial where I hoped to see Demi. She wasn't there, and one of the other girls told me it was her night off. While Kyle ordered our beers, I took a moment to send Demi a text.

'Hi! How R U?' I am getting cooler by the second.

"How you getting along?" I asked Kyle.

"Getting by," Kyle responded. "Bitch keeps texting, saying she wants to talk."

"Shit," I said.

"That your new favourite word?" He asked. "I see you've joined the modern world," he said, nodding toward my phone.

We exchanged cell numbers, and Kyle chided me for buying an iPhone, going on for quite some time about how much better an Android is. I nodded and grunted in response several times throughout his tirade. I had absolutely no idea what he was talking about.

"So, who were these assholes?" Kyle asked.

I gave him the Reader's Digest version of everything that had happened, from buying the penthouse to my last conversation with Bouchard. I left out all of the 'flashes' and time control parts, of course.

"Where'd you learn to fight, Max?"

177

"Just natural talent, I guess," I responded. "Good reflexes."

"We should just call up your friends 'The Rebellion' and go beat the hell out of Bouchard and his little bullies."

"It's 'Rebellion'," I said. "No 'The'."

"Who cares?"

"They do," I said, shrugging. "We have to find out how Bouchard gets the girls out of the country, assuming they go out of the country, and who he sells them to. And we need to find proof, so the cops can put them away?"

"Tell me why this is your problem again."

"I can't let this kind of stuff go on in my city," I said.

"Your city?" Kyle asked, incredulously. "You've lived here three months! You've had too many people tell you, you look like that superhero! It's gone to your head!"

We talked a bit more about Kyle's wife, 'That Fucking Bitch', and her friend, 'That Son-of-a-Bitch', and how Kyle was feeling about it all. He seemed to be getting along pretty well, all things considered, probably because he had no compunctions about venting. He vented loudly and often, with no consideration for who was sitting close by and what they might think. Kyle's unabashed honesty and general lack of concern with what strangers thought of him were some of his most entertaining qualities. We finished our second beer and Kyle insisted on paying for them. It was important to him that I know our friendship had nothing to do with my lottery winnings.

I had been watching my phone throughout our visit hoping that Demi would respond to my text. It took all of my willpower to keep from going to her apartment to make sure she was okay. I had just walked into my apartment when my cell buzzed.

'Good. You?' It was Demi. I was very relieved.

'I'm good. Can I call you in the morning?'

My phone rang almost immediately.

"Hi," I said.

"Hi," Demi said. "Sorry I took so long to respond. I was having a bath, and my phone was in the other room."

"No worries," I lied. "I wanted to make sure you were okay. Those people I got involved with down at the nightclub have been threatening me. Telling me they'll hurt people I care about. They beat up Kyle today."

"What? Kyle? How many guys?"

Kyle and Demi had met the first time I brought the team to the bar and they hit-it-off immediately. Together they enjoyed poking fun at me and laughing at the way I talk. Have I mentioned...? Oh, forget it!

"Two. These guys are tough, armed and very dangerous," I said. "You need to be very careful. Make sure your doors are locked and call me right away if you think you're in any danger."

"My hero," Demi said.

"I'm serious, Demi. These are bad people."

"I'll be careful."

I was about to tell her I might have to go on a date with another girl but that it was only to make sure that she, too, was safe from Bouchard when Demi continued in a different tone of voice. Probably a good thing. I'd have been opening a can of worms I wasn't prepared to eat.

"Max," Demi said.

"Yeah," I said.

"It's too bad I didn't have my phone with me before. It might have been fun talking to you while I was in the tub."

"Oh," I said. I was instantly sweating more than I had during the entire rugby game.

'My God, Elsie! This girl is killing me!'

'Old Goat!'

"Ni-night," Demi said.

I went straight in and had another James Bond Shower. I skipped the hot water part.

CHAPTER TWENTY

The next morning, Detective Corporal Tkatchuk called, asking me to join him at the RCMP Building in the south end of the city for a ten o'clock meeting. It was another beautiful autumn morning, made fresher by the light rain the previous evening. As I sat in the parking lot waiting for the detective, I looked around at the new cars in the surrounding auto dealership lots. I wonder if having the RCMP offices located amidst the Auto Mall is a theft and vandalism deterrent. Probably not. The Corporal arrived with three minutes to spare, and we walked in together.

Sergeant Richard Smith, Rick, was a forty-ish balding man who was probably in great shape not long ago, but was starting to show the results of desk work and a fast-food diet. He shook hands with me, no flash thank God, and then with young Tkatchuk.

"Rumour has it, you were promoted to prove the City likes Fags," the Mountie said to the City Cop.

Holy Cow! I thought.

The younger cop smiled and said, "Fuck you, too!"

The older cop chuckled as we all sat down.

"As I told Cory on the phone, the Powers-That-Be, what's left of them anyway, have deemed it necessary that we have a man assigned to Saskatoon's missing women problem. I'm the man, so if either of you knows of a good apartment for rent, let me know. I'm not moving my family here until things in the force settle down some."

As I had learned from the morning paper, the RCMP were in the midst of a significant staffing and management upheaval. The National Inquiry into Missing and Murdered Indigenous Women and Girls had brought to head an issue that politicians and law enforcement organizations had swept under the rug for decades. The resulting attention had shaken up the RCMP in particular, and many high ranking officials were either dismissed or suspended pending a major internal investigation.

"I know a few of the guys downtown own rental properties," Corey said. "Probably better if you stop in and check out the bulletin board yourself. You'll get treated better if you don't tell anyone that you and I are such good buddies."

"Thanks! I will. So, what has Saskatoon's one-man force investigating murdered and missing women managed to accomplish without my help?" He made it sound like he was joking, but it still came across like he was pretty self-important.

Cory laughed without mirth and proceeded to fill Rick in on his frustrations at being blocked by his own organization and ended by accounting my experience at WonderWall nightclub and my meeting with Bouchard. At the mention of Bouchard, the older cop's eyebrows went up, and he nodded, giving the impression that he'd heard the name before. The younger cop neglected to mention his Chief's unique problems.

"I'm not at liberty to discuss what I know about the department's internal shakeup, not that I know shit anyway, but I will say that Bouchard's name has come up more than once. It seems he has a knack for getting involved where he shouldn't be able to get involved. I'm waiting to hear back from a contact in Quebec who's looking into his 'involvement' out there."

"Bouchard's a bastard alright," Cory said. "And his muscle are a tough bunch of pricks. Even the local gangs are keeping their distance."

The younger cop then told the Mountie about my trip to Montreal and described the approach that Matthew, Daniel and I were taking, tracking Bouchard's people electronically. Smith looked mildly surprised and amused at this, and I wondered if there wasn't a law against using trackers that way.

"I have to say, you don't look like the type to be pals with The Rebellion," Rick said, addressing me. I didn't bother correcting him. Another time. Maybe.

"I've been forced to rethink my opinion on them," I said. "It seems they really just want to keep their people safe and keep their kids out of the hands of other gangs."

"Every criminal thinks he's uniquely justified in his actions," Sergeant Smith said. It sounded strangely familiar. "I wouldn't be surprised if these guys are selling their own sisters and blaming it on Bouchard."

I bristled and sat forward in my chair.

"I think the biggest problem with your investigations is that you've all got your minds made up before you put your badge on in the morning!" I could probably have said that a little quieter.

"Hang on, Lone Ranger. I'm just saying I've never known a gang that didn't have some serious shit going on. Illegal shit."

That didn't calm me down any, but it did bring a smile to the younger cops face. I wasn't getting the best vibe from the RCMP officer, and I didn't I like him very much. I wanted to argue with the guy, but it would serve no real purpose. I thought, instead, about introducing him to Gabriel. That made me feel better.

"Okay, well, I'm going to spend a little time getting settled here and then maybe I'll go talk to this Herny Bouchard. I'll also be talking with these Rebellion friends of yours. I'll let you know if I hear anything back from my guy in Quebec, Corey. And, Mr. Campbell, you should probably step back from all of this and let Corporal Tkatchuk and I handle things from here on."

"That arrogant Son-of-a-Bitch!" I'd managed to hold it in until we were back out in the parking lot.

Corporal Tkatchuk chuckled a little.

"Don't let him get under your skin, Max. He didn't say anything I didn't expect."

"I wanted to punch him in the head."

"Really? I couldn't tell. In fact, I think I want to play poker with you. Bring lots of money." Corey's smile cheered me up a little. "Give the guy a chance. He'll lighten up once he's found his footing around here. In the meantime, he might be able to do things that I haven't been able to do, like put some pressure on Bouchard."

"I guess. Bouchard's guys beat up a friend of mine last night," I said, changing the subject. "I didn't feel like bringing it up in front of Sergeant Dick-Face."

I told Corey what happened and the message they'd given Kyle.

"Make sure your friends have nine-one-one on their speed dials. Anyway, I don't understand why Bouchard thinks he can get you to work for him. What good would you be to him?"

"The bastard just likes to control everyone around him, is my guess," I responded. It was a safer answer than 'He thinks I can solve all his problems with my super-speed'.

Back in my truck, I gave Jenny a call. When she didn't answer, I left a message for her to call me back as soon as she could. I wasn't comfortable pursuing her so aggressively, but she was my biggest worry at the moment. I was heading down Clarence Street on my way downtown when she called back. I hung a right on Temperance and parked before answering.

"Max, what is it?" Jenny sounded apprehensive and maybe a bit irritated.

"Sorry it took so long to answer. I was driving," I said, trying to sound laid back.

"Can't you Bluetooth to your car?"

I had no idea what that meant, so I ignored it.

"I'm sorry for being a pain, Jenny, but is there any chance you're free this evening?"

"Sorry, Max, but I'm working again this evening." She seemed somewhat exasperated.

"Oh. Okay. Another time then?"

"Sure, Max. Bye."

"Bye."

I got the distinct impression that the next time I called, she wouldn't be picking up.

I had dropped Aaron with Matthew before meeting with the cops, and she was sitting with him when I got back to Starbucks.

"Anything new?" I asked.

"The vehicles we've tagged have gone nowhere important. Daniel is sending boys to Bouchard's office and the warehouse to put trackers on more vehicles."

"Let's go somewhere for lunch, Aaron. Not here, though. I can't afford it," I said. "Matthew, would you like to join us?"

"No, thank you, Orville. I must remain where I can

monitor things."

Aaron and I strolled leisurely over to the Midtown Plaza. It had been quite a while since we'd walked together, and our surroundings reminded me of the first time we'd come this way. Wow, how things had changed in a very short time. That morning my new body was barely a day old, and I was constantly aware of how amazing it felt to be young again. Recently, I'd been finding that several hours could go by when I'd completely forget I'd ever been a ninety-one-year-old man. Those first couple of days, my biggest worry was if I'd have enough money to get by until I managed to find a job. Forty million dollars later and I was soon to reside in the penthouse suite of Saskatoon's newest residential development, assuming the building gets finished after we put the developer in prison. Back then, I worried I'd never manage to catch up to a world where technology infests every facet of life. Now? Well, okay. Maybe not everything had changed.

"What's Bluetooth?" I asked.

"Bluetooth is a way to make wireless connections between electronic devices," Aaron said. "Why?"

"I was in my truck, and I'd pulled over to talk on the cell, and the person I was talking to said, 'Can't you Bluetooth to your stereo?'"

"Oh yeah! I'll have to show you how to connect it so you can talk hands-free while you drive."

"I think I talk 'hands-free' all the time."

"Not funny, Max."

"Still. That sounds pretty amazing!"

"Bluetooth? It's been around forever."

"No," I said. "No, it hasn't."

When we got back to Starbucks, Matthew was on his phone and again, furiously typing on one of his laptops.

"What's up?" Aaron asked.

"Keep me posted," he said into his cell and then broke the connection. "There's been some activity around the warehouse. They've pulled in another semi, and some guys are working inside its trailer. I'm having one of Daniel's men take a drone over there, so I can try to get a look at what they're doing."

A short time later we sat watching Matthew's screen as the drone-mounted camera showed us the roof of the warehouse and the semi-trailers parked there. Matthew appeared to be controlling the drone from his computer.

"How are you controlling that?" I asked.

"I'm connected to it through Jeff's cell phone on site," Matthew said.

"Wow. I didn't know people could do that," I said.

Matthew glanced briefly up at me and then back down to his laptop.

"People can't. I can," Matthew said, dryly. "Unfortunately, because the trailer's backed up to a warehouse door I can't get an angle that shows us anything."

"Those are swing doors on that trailer. They'll have to pull away from the loading dock to close them. If you are ready, you might be able to see in then."

"I'll be ready," Matthew said, glancing up at me. His tone of voice was reserved, but his eyes were hard, and I felt I'd been chastised.

He's a bit of an irritable prick today.

"Matthew, I'd like your opinion on something," I said. "I'm feeling like I'm being pulled in too many directions. I want to be ready to move if it looks like we can take action with Bouchard and his thugs, but at the same time, with him threatening my friends, I feel like I need to keep an eye on all of them. I can't do everything at once."

"I've been thinking about that as well. It's doubtful Bouchard realized that Aaron is one of the young women you rescued from Wonderwall the other night. However, it seems unlikely he wouldn't know you have a young roommate since he's obviously been having you watched. I've spoken with Daniel about it, and we think it's best she stays at the house until we deal with Bouchard and his men."

"Hey!" Aaron said. "Don't I get a say in this?"

"No!" Matthew and I responded in unison.

"How well do you know Daniel?" I asked Aaron, as we drove back to our apartment. She was playing with my phone and my truck stereo as we talked.

"Not very well."

"How well does he know you?"

"What do you mean?" Aaron asked.

"Does he know you as Aaron the boy, or Aaron the girl, or both."

Aaron giggled. "I think he knows that boy and girl are both me, but, to be honest, I'm not certain."

"So, are you going there as a boy or a girl?"

A boy, I guess. What's your point?"

"Well, what if he puts you in a room with another boy?" I asked. "Or a bunch of boys?"

"O-oh! Well then, maybe I'll get to see some boys running around naked!" She said, laughing.

Did I mention I don't care for being laughed at?

"Why don't you make yourself useful and 'Bluetooth' my phone to the truck?" I asked.

At the apartment, I played with my phone and waited impatiently while Aaron had a 'quick bath'. By the time she was done, Bouchard had had of time to murder everyone I knew and abducted forty more girls.

When I dropped her off at Rebellion House, she jumped from the truck, backpack in hand, and ran up to Gabriel, giving him a big hug. As he hugged her back, he again used his hate-ray vision to peel the paint off the side of my truck. Didn't he know we were on the same side?

As I drove away, I tested my new Bluetooth connection and gave Kyle a call. I was happy to learn that Marcus, another rugby buddy, was with him. Marcus was thinking about moving in, so Kyle was taking him to see the house. Marcus was one of the smaller guys on the team, but he was fast and sturdy. I didn't think anyone was likely to challenge Kyle when he had someone like Marcus to watch his back. However, it wasn't Kyle that I was most worried about.

"Max! Are you stalking me?" Demi asked as she flew past with a tray full of drinks.

"Yes," I said.

The bar was busy, even for a Friday evening, and I was forced to take a seat at the bar. I was totally okay with that, as it gave me the best vantage point from which to admire Demi. Out of the corner of my eye, I noticed three familiar figures at a table not far away.

"Should I tell them you'd like to join them?" Demi chided as she cleared her tray of empty glasses. I could feel their eyes on me, making the hair on the back of my neck stand up.

"If I bought them a round of drinks do you think the skinny one would be my date for the prom?"

"Why the skinny one? Is it all about appearance with you?"

I looked Demi up and down, smiled broadly and said, "Yup. Could be!"

The young lady tending bar, I think her name was Ashley, set a Great Western Light in front of me and said, "Girls have brains too, you know, Max."

"Not required," I said.

Both girls groaned, and Demi took another load of drinks out to her tables.

I had learned on one of my first visits to the bar that Demi really did have brains, and was currently studying for combined computer and electrical engineering degrees. With those under her belt, she intended to then enter the physical engineering department. I'd known a lot of smart people over the years, but she was in a class of her own. I reminded myself, not for the first time, that I'd have to reread Stephen Hawking's A Brief History of Time.

Demi returned from dropping beer at the cougars' table.

"I told them those were from you. I also told them you were mine, so you're safe for now."

"Thanks!" That made me happier than it probably should have. "Speaking of brains, Brain, how're your classes going?"

"Good. Busy!"

"Demi says she's going to develop antigravity," Ashley said.

Demi slipped past, holding her tray high above her head.

"From where I sit, I'd say she's already done that!" I said.

"What? Oh yeah! Boobs *and* brains! I hate her!" Ashley said, a mock frown on her face.

Another waitress, who had been listening in, took that as an opportunity to join the conversation.

"You should see her naked! They're amazing!"

"Janet, you Lez!" Ashley laughed.

"Not me! I like boys! But I'd switch for Demi!"

Everyone laughed at that except me. Instead, my always active imagination went on a little side trip and the mental picture the conversation inspired caused my face to go red. I could feel myself starting to heat up. I don't recall Orville being so inclined to blush. I tried picturing the three cougars naked. It helped, and my face started to cool.

"Oh look! He's blushing!" Ashley said. "You're so sweet, Max."

"Quit flirting with Max, Ashley," Demi said as she headed away with more drinks.

I ate dinner enjoying the warm, happy feeling that comes in

the presence of good people. It seemed Demi had forgiven me for my previous thoughtlessness. Having her say I was hers made me so happy I spent most of the evening grinning like an idiot. By the end of the night, my cheeks hurt.

"When are you off?" I asked Demi a while later.

"When it slows down enough. It's Friday, so it'll likely be elevenish."

"Can I carry your books home from school?"

"I have my car here, Max," she said, smiling.

"I just want to make sure you get home safe."

"You're really that worried?"

"Can I follow you home? Otherwise, I'm not going to get any sleep tonight."

"You follow me home, and you might not get any sleep anyway."

She left with more drinks before seeing my face turn a new, more intense shade of red. Ashley looked over at me and laughed. Okay, sometimes I'm totally fine with being laughed at.

I spent the rest of the evening sipping beer very slowly, eating way too many appetizers, watching sports on the screens and chatting with the staff and other customers. It was a heck of a good night.

When we got to Demi's I walked her up to her apartment.

"Okay, Hero, I'm home safe," she said. "Would you like to come in for a drink?"

"I better not," I said slowly, my face turning only a little red this time.

"Okay, Handsome. Thanks for looking out for me!"

She reached over and, taking me by the chin, gave me a kiss like I hadn't had in over fifty years.

'Don't look, Elsie!'

Turning away and heading back to my truck might have

been one of the hardest things I'd ever done. Still, it was a heck of a good night.

CHAPTER TWENTY-ONE

"Orville."

"Matthew." I set his preferred coffee concoction in front of him. "Any news?"

"I did manage to get a look inside the trailer."

Matthew spun one of his laptops around so I could see the image on the screen. It showed the back end of a semi-trailer with its doors open as seen from just slightly above the warehouse roof. It appeared to be a normal empty trailer.

"Looks normal," I said.

Matthew nodded and said, "Which it shouldn't."

"Huh?"

"They spent several hours hauling construction materials into that trailer and doing some kind of work on it."

"Oh, I see what you're saying," I said. "An awful lot of effort to end up with a normal empty trailer. So, you're thinking they rebuilt the trailer to hide something in it."

"My guess is they built a false front. It's not easy to see from this angle, but it appears to me that the inside front wall of that trailer is a bit too close to the back end, considering the length of the overall unit."

"A room for transporting human cargo."

"Agreed," Matthew said.

"I think it's time I go take a look at this warehouse. I'm tired of sitting around waiting for something to happen."

"Agreed," Matthew said. "Should I ask Daniel to meet you there with some of his guys?"

"Nah," I answered. "I like to work alone."

I was heading down 2nd avenue, leaving downtown when my phone rang. I answered, tapping the screen on my dashboard.

"Max here," I said, feeling like technology and I were finally starting to see eye to eye, or maybe eye to screen.

"Max. It's Matthew." Did he call me Max?

"What's up?"

"They're moving the trailer. It'll be gone before you get there."

"Dang-it!"

"It's not a problem. I had our guy there put a tracker on it. I just thought you might want to know before you got there."

"Thanks. I'm going to stop in and look around anyway. Would your guy there like a coffee or anything?"

"I think he would. Pick up an Extra Large Double Double and leave it on the box of your truck."

"Will do."

"Max."

"Yeah?"

"Thank you."

"Yeah."

I swung by Tim Horton's.

As I pulled up across the street from the warehouse on Miner's Avenue, I saw a man closing a large overhead door from the inside. I hopped out of the truck, put the Tim's on the truck box, and headed across the street.

"We're closed," a man's voice said the moment I stepped inside.

"No problem, buddy. I'm just here to ask you a few questions."

"Got no answers for you." Just a hint of a French accent.

"We'll see," I said. I gazed around the large open, empty room to see if I could spot any cameras. I didn't see any, but that didn't mean they weren't there.

What functioning warehouse is this empty? I thought.

"Why's your warehouse so empty?" I asked. "Business hurting?"

"Fuck off," replied the man, walking toward me. I looked him over, and finding no bruises, decided he hadn't met Gabriel the other day.

"What do you guys ship from this place anyway?"

"Fuck off!"

"That doesn't sound very profitable to me. Probably why business is hurting."

"Think you're funny, Asshole?"

"Possibly not, but I am polite. Something you might consider." I was having way too much fun with this.

He tried to shove me, and I pushed time, stepping just out of the way and causing him to stumble forward. This shoving thing must have been taught in the Bouchard Army's Basic Training. In normal time I slapped him on the back of the head as he went by. Way too much fun!

"You fucking asshole!" he yelled at me.

"I'll ask you again. What do you ship here?"

He looked like he wanted to punch me but changed his mind and began walking toward the office. I pushed time just long enough to step in front of him. He almost ran into me and recoiled like he'd bounced off a wall.

"Fuck!" he said. He didn't seem to be having as much fun as I was.

"Answer my questions before I start getting pissed off. You won't like that," I said, trying to sound ominous. "Try this one. Who's your boss?"

He turned like he was going to head for the door I'd come in through. I was suddenly in front of him again. Still fun, but it was starting to run thin.

"Jesus Christ, man! How…" He let his question hang.

I gave him a two handed push. He was a little smaller than me and not nearly as fit. He staggered backward. I caught him from behind and kept him on his feet, then was suddenly in front of him again.

"Who owns this place?" I barked at him. "Tell me before I put you in the hospital!"

"Monsieur Bouchard," the man spat, finally coming to his senses.

What are you distributing here?"

"Nothing. We just moved in"

"The trailer that just left here. Where was it going?" I know that we had a tracker on it, but we were starting to get along so well I just wanted to keep the conversation moving.

"I don't know," he spat.

"Where's Bouchard?"

"I don't know."

"Where does he live?"

The man hesitated, so I leaned toward him a bit.

"He'll fucking kill me, man." He seemed genuinely upset.

"Where?" I screamed at him.

"He's got an acreage South of town."

"Where?"

He winced like I was going to hit him. I hadn't moved a muscle. Honest.

"South of town, man! I don't know where." He was pretty spooked. He didn't know.

"I turned and walked toward the exit."

"Tell your boss I said 'Hi'," I said. His boss was not going to be happy with him.

Back outside I noticed that the coffee was gone from the truck box. I hopped inside, turned the truck around and headed for circle drive. I tapped the screen on the dash.

"Call Brad the Salesman"

"Calling 'Brad the Salesman', mobile," the creepy female voice said.

The voice that answered sounded more than a little groggy. Brad had had a late night.

"Yeah, Brad here."

"Brad! It's Max."

"Max! Hey! How are ya? What can I do for you?"

It's nice when just the mention of your name creates so much excitement.

"Brad! I'm supposed to be meeting your boss out at his place, and I guess I've got the directions mixed up. Can you help me out?"

"Uh, yeah! I guess. Uh, did you turn at the S.I.R. sign?"

"Yeah, but I must have gone too far," I lied.

"Uh let me think. I'm pretty sure it's the second turn. Yeah, take the second left, and his place is about a mile in."

"Number twenty-three, right?"

"Uh, no. No, I'm pretty sure it's forty-seven."

"Oh, yeah! That's right! Thanks, Brad. Gotta go. I'm pretty late!" I tapped the screen.

'Not bad, hey, Elsie?'

'I always knew you had potential!'

When I saw the sign for Saskatchewan International Raceway, I turned off the road and watched for the second turn. I was fortunate there were only roads heading left or I would not have known which way to turn. The area was slightly hilly, with enough natural brush and tree growth to provide each lot with plenty of privacy. I pulled off the road when I saw a sign for Lot 45 and walked the short distance to Bouchard's property. As I entered the yard, I saw a huge two-story house with an attached garage. A newer model Honda Civic was parked in the driveway. Behind the house was a large Quonset made of shiny corrugated metal.

I pushed at time and jogged over to the ugly metal building and returned to regular time as I looked through the window of a large overhead door. The interior was dark, so I tried the knob on a smaller man-sized door. It was unlocked and opened quietly. I listened for a moment and, hearing nothing, stepped inside. I gave my eyes time to adjust to the lower light level and found a mostly empty storage area. Nothing suspicious. I stepped back out and jogged over to the house.

One of the nice things about Saskatchewan's small population is that it's kept the crime rate comparatively low, so many people don't bother to lock their doors. That'll probably change with people like Bouchard coming around. Once inside, I gently closed the door behind me and found myself looking at a large open interior comprised of a kitchen, dining area, and a spacious section with several couches. Seeing no one about, I walked to a large carpeted staircase and silently headed up.

As I reached the top, I could hear music playing faintly

from a room at the end of a wide hallway. As I got closer, I heard the hissing of a shower. I took a deep breath and stepped through the large French Doors prepared to face the monster within.

I was not prepared for what I actually found.

CHAPTER TWENTY-TWO

"Jenny!" I exclaimed.

The half-naked girl with the dragonfly tattoo screamed in sudden terror and jumped up from the bed. She turned in midair, covering her breasts with one arm and holding out the other as if to ward off the devil. As she landed on her feet her eyes grew wide with recognition, and she said, "Max!"

"Jenny?"

"Max?"

"What the...Jenny, where's Bouchard?"

"Max? What are you doing here? You know Henry?"

At this point, a naked, wet girl came bounding out of an adjoining room, a towel held in front of her in a failed attempt to cover herself.

"What the fuck, Jenny!" She exclaimed. Then, from the corner of her eye, she spotted me and screamed like a banshee.

"JesusFuckingChrist!Whothefuckareyou?" she blurted, one great big word.

"This is Max. Max. What the fuck? What are you doing here?"

"Jenny! Are you okay? Where's Bouchard?"

"I can't believe you know Henry! This is crazy. Go wash the soap out of your hair, Becky!"

The naked girl dropped the arm holding the towel, it wasn't hiding anything anyway, and went back into the bathroom. I looked back at Jenny who had picked up a bra from the floor in front of her and was casually putting it on. She seemed totally unconcerned with her nudity in front of a relatively new acquaintance. Mind you, it was a little late now to be concerned about it.

"This is so crazy," Jenny said again and before I had a chance to ask again, said, "Henry left a little while ago."

"Are you okay?" I asked. "What's going on?"

Jenny had donned a shirt that she'd also found on the floor and turned to cross to a dresser on the other side of the room. As she picked up a large wad of bills, she turned back to me with a slightly embarrassed smile.

"I told you I had another job," she said, and then after an awkward pause, "So, how do you know Henry?"

A huge gaping space was opening up in my abdomen, just under my heart, and I was having a hard time drawing in a breath. The room seemed to be spinning a bit and the bright sunlight coming in through two large windows made the entire scene seem oddly overexposed.

"Uh, I, uh just bought a suite in his development. The penthouse."

"Really! That's awesome!" Jenny seemed totally at ease now that she'd gotten over being startled.

The other girl, Becky, came back into the room with one towel around her and using another to dry her hair. She picked up clothes from the floor and tossed them on the bed. I stood there staring as she dropped both towels and began getting dressed. She was exceptionally well put together. I knew I should look away, but I had pretty much relinquished all conscious control of my body.

"How do you two know each other then?" Becky asked casually as she stepped into what looked like a headband but turned out to be a skirt.

"Max and I just met the other day."

"He's pretty cute, Jen. Wanna share him?"

The girls chatted back and forth as Becky finished dressing, occasionally asking a question of me. I think I answered. As we all moved downstairs and out to the driveway, it slowly sunk in that Becky was serious about an invitation to join them at their place in the city, and Jenny seemed accepting and excited about it. As the girls opened the doors of the Civic, I began making my way slowly down the drive to the main road.

"Where are you going?" one of them called.

"I parked out here," my body answered.

"Are you coming to our place?" one of them asked.

"No. I guess not," my body answered.

They honked the horn as they drove past and then they were gone, not knowing what they had done to a saddened and very tired old man.

As I walked back to the truck I felt like screaming at the ever-changing world for ever changing in ways I never thought it should, but I wasn't able to draw a breath deep enough. I wanted to cry, but in that shocked and saddened state, I didn't feel a strong enough connection with my new body to make any tears flow. I wanted to get sick and maybe force the empty ache I was feeling up and out of my chest, but I couldn't. And for the first time since I began this remarkable new life, I wanted to go back in time to where I was just a broken body hanging from the bloodied seatbelt of an overturned car in a lonely ditch. But I couldn't.

I'm not sure how long I sat in my truck before pulling it out of the ditch and heading back to town, but I had just made it back onto Highway 11 when my phone rang.

"Yeah," I heard my voice say.

"Max, its Aaron."

"Yeah."

"Gabriel's sister's gone missing! All Hell's breaking loose around here!"

You know, it's funny. Sometimes life throws so much garbage at you that you start thinking that it's nothing but a big ball of crap, and then something even worse happens and you realize that life ain't so bad after all.

"Shit!" I had to say something to get her to keep talking.

"He got a phone call from his mother and freaked out. He took one of the cars. Daniel's taken some guys and gone after him."

"Where's he gone?"

"We're not sure, and we can't call him 'cause he smashed his phone when he was freaking. We think he's going to the warehouse."

"There was only one guy there earlier. If they don't stop him, he'll kill the guy."

"Where are you? Aaron asked.

"Just heading back into town. Hold on. I think I'm getting another call." There was an intermittent beeping coming from my speakers.

"I'll hang up, so you can answer it. Call me back."

I started to pull to the side of the road and glanced at the screen on the dash as I went to tap the answer icon. It changed the instant I looked, but I thought I had seen Demi's name displayed there before it switched to the standard radio configuration. I slammed on the brakes and skidded to a stop and pulled my phone out of my back pocket. I was shaking as I hit the power button and searched the screen for signs of a missed call. It took a few seconds of fumbling before I decided to just call her. Holding the phone up to my ear I just about jumped out of my skin when the ringing came over the truck's speakers, many times louder than I'd expected. The ringing continued. Demi didn't answer.

Assuming she walked away from her cell when I hadn't answered, I dropped the phone on the passenger seat and pulled away from the side of the road, at the same time tapping the dash screen.

"Call Daniel, Mobile," I said, just as a shockingly loud horn from a passing semi expressed the driver's displeasure at my having cut him off.

"Gall-darned cell phones!" I spat.

"What?" Daniel answered.

"Sorry," I said. "What's going on?"

"Gabriel's sister is missing."

"I know. Aaron told me. Where are you?"

"Bouchard's warehouse. We followed Gabriel here. There's no one here. When Gabriel's done breaking shit, we're going to try to get him back to the house."

"Good luck with that," I said.

"Where are you?"

"Just coming into the city. I found out where Bouchard lives, so I went to check it out."

I went silent, thinking about what I found at Bouchard's.

"And?" Daniel inquired.

"Sorry. Nothing there," I lied. "Have any of your guys seen anything."

"Nothing's happening at Bouchard's office either. His pricks were spotted out prowling around last night, though."

"Something's up. Do we know where the trailer went?"

"I'm sure Matthew knows, but I can't reach him."

"Where is he?"

Daniel paused before answering.

"It's Saturday. He's probably at home. I've left a message for him to call."

"Okay. Let me know if anything changes. I have to call Aaron back."

"Later," Daniel said and ended the call.

I thought about Matthew, mostly so I wouldn't think about my great-granddaughter. I realized I really knew nothing about the man, other than he was a twin and he was crippled. For some reason the manager of the 2nd Avenue Starbucks let him use one of their tables as an office. There, he provided his unusual tech services. That was it. It didn't give me much to ponder, actually.

I was soon on Circle drive heading toward the west side of the city. After making sure that I was aware of all the traffic around me, I tapped the screen and said, "Call Aaron, mobile."

It took a few rings before Aaron picked up.

"Max," she said.

"What's happening?"

"Nothing. I think Daniel and the guys are bringing Gabriel back. Have you talked to Matthew?"

"No. You?"

"No."

"Have you eaten?"

"No."

"I'll be there right away. We'll go eat."

We sat in an isolated booth in the Grainfields Family Restaurant on Circle Drive. The girl in boys clothing sat quietly and listened while I told her of my trip to Bouchard's acreage.

Her eyes grew wide when I reached the part when I found my favourite great-grandchild conducting business in the home of the evilest man I've ever known. We both sat quietly for a few minutes after I finished my tale. I've always liked how Aaron takes time to let things sink in before commenting.

"How are you?" she asked, just as the waitress came up behind her to take our order.

The mild flirtations of the server, giggling a little too much and touching my arm for no reason at all, something I'd gotten used to in recent weeks and usually found amusing, were intensely irritating today and I wanted to tell her to just get our gall-darned food.

"How are you?" Aaron asked again when the waitress finally went away.

"I'm okay, I guess. It's not the first time I've found out someone wasn't who I thought she was."

That caused Aaron to give me a small smile that allowed the girl inside the boy to peek out.

"You know, before Elsie and I started our family, I imagined what it would be like to have kids. Then we had kids, and as they grew up, I learned that they were born with their own ideas about who they were going to be and how they were going to act. They were perfectly normal little people, but they weren't the mini-Elsie and mini-Orville I had thought they would be. I loved them with all my heart, but it took two more generations before I felt like I'd had a child that I really connected with."

A wave of sadness overcame me, and I had to stop talking for a bit. Aaron waited patiently.

"The world has changed in so many ways since I was this age the first time. The world I grew up in was innocent. Nobody's innocent anymore. Some days it feels as if the entire world is a child that doesn't act the way I believe it should. I guess I have to learn to accept that it's not the nineteen-forties. A lot of things get easier as you get older. Accepting change is not one of them."

The waitress brought our food, and I avoided looking up in hopes that she'd just leave the food and go away. It didn't work. The girl touched my shoulder to get my attention and asked if there was anything else we needed.

"Jesus," I said, in mild exasperation after she left.

"You can't blame her, you know. You really are incredibly hot!"

"Jesus!" I said, a bit more emphatically. "I suppose there's really nothing wrong with a girl making extra money entertaining rich guys. I've always thought it was strange that it's illegal to sell something when it's totally legal to give it away."

"I know other girls that make money that way. For white girls, it's relatively safe. They can do it just by hanging out in hotel bars, and nobody cares. Native girls in hotel bars are not usually made to feel welcome, so they end up working the streets, and they can't do that without one of the gangs offering to 'protect' them. If they weren't doing drugs to begin with, the gangs push them into it and next thing you know the gangs own them. It's bullshit."

"Still, I can't help but worry for Jenny's safety. Especially knowing that she does business with scum like Bouchard."

"Bouchard won't do anything to a white girl like your great-granddaughter. She's got a job, friends, a family. People who would go looking if something happened to her. More importantly, the cops will pay attention to the people in her world if something happened to her."

I ate some of my food thinking how most of us are privileged in ways we don't even realize. Privilege never walks up and smacks you in the face the way a lack of privilege regularly does. Obviously, there must be some neurons misfiring in my head when the subject of where my great-granddaughter can work her prostitution job has me recollecting how privileged I've been.

"I guess I have to accept that she knows what she's doing. And it seems that she doesn't actually work alone. I know for a fact that wasn't an unusual situation for her."

"How do you know that?" Aaron asked.

"No flash," I said around a mouthful of food. "I shook her hand a couple of days ago, and I got nothing. If she was frightened, or traumatized, or even overly excited, I would have gotten some kind of vision of the event. Obviously, it was more exciting for Bouchard than it was for her."

We ate our food in silence for a bit.

Then Aaron said, "I wonder if there isn't something unique about how intensely Bouchard enjoys these encounters. I wonder if it doesn't say something about his psyche."

"What do you mean?"

"Well, it's not likely, considering the business that Creep is in, that Bouchard doesn't enjoy a lot of kinky little trysts."

"Yeah."

"So, two times you've come in contact with him and both times you've gotten one of your 'flashes'. So, is it possible that he experiences things like that more intensely than normal people? Is that maybe why people like him get involved in shit like that? Is that part of a psychopath's personality?"

For a woman only eighteen years old, Aaron has a very mature and thoughtful way of looking at things. When she says something like that while dressed in her twelve-year-old-boy persona, it kind of freaks me out.

"That's a really good question," I said. "Anyways, let's get…"

"Stop right there!" Aaron cut me off in mid-sentence.

"What?" I asked.

"You did it again. You said 'enna-ways'. It's not 'enna-ways' it's 'anyway'."

I tried to restrain the mild irritation I felt at that. After all, I had asked her to help me modernize the way I talk.

"Any-way," I said carefully, "I want to give Matthew a call, but I don't want to do it in here."

Matthew picked up on the third ring.

"Max." I guess on the phone I'm not Orville.

"Where are you?" I asked.

"I'm at home. Where are you?"

"Aaron and I just had lunch. I'm going to run her back to Rebellion House."

"Rebellion House? I like that," Matthew said. "I think Daniel would love it."

It hadn't occurred to me that I had given their headquarters a name. It was just how I'd come to think of it.

"What's happening?" I asked.

"I've tracked the trailer to a garage in Dundurn. Daniel is getting some men together…"

"Sorry, Matthew, I've got another call coming in. Can I call you back?"

"I'll put you on hold. Hang on," Aaron said, tapping on the dash screen.

"Hello?" a voice said.

I hadn't realized we were connected already.

"Yeah, Max here," I said.

"Mr. Campbell." the voice said.

It was Bouchard.

CHAPTER TWENTY-THREE

At the sound of Bouchard's voice, my heart tried to jump out of my chest.

"What do you want, Bouchard?"

"It appears you are a very resourceful young man. That's good. I like my people to be resourceful."

"I am not one of 'your people', Bouchard."

"We'll see, Mr. Campbell. We'll see."

"What do you want, Bouchard?" I repeated.

"I have a little job for you, Mr. Campbell."

It was amazing how that guy could make me hate my name!

"I don't work for you, Bouchard!"

"We'll see. There are some Indians causing problems at one

of my facilities. I need you to go over there and take care of them for me."

"Fuck you, Bouchard. Take care of your own problems."

"You will take care of this problem for me, Mr. Campbell, if you care about this pretty little waitress here as much as I think you do."

My heart started pounding so hard that I could hear it pulsing in my ears. It almost drowned out the sound of muffled screaming coming from the truck speakers.

"Are you there, Mr. Campbell?"

"I'm going to kill you, you bastard."

"You are going to go to my warehouse, Mr. Campbell. Miner's Avenue and sixty-third street. You are going to go there and make those Indians go away." He sounded so smugly confident. "You have excellent taste in women, Mr. Campbell. This young woman of yours is very pretty."

There was more muffled screaming before the line went dead.

"Matthew, are you there?" Aaron said while I was still trying to come to grips with the situation.

"Yes, Aaron."

"Do you know where Bouchard is right now?"

"I'm afraid not. We weren't able to get a tracker on his personal vehicle."

"Does Daniel have men at the warehouse on Miner's?" I asked.

"I don't believe so. Why?"

"Matthew, can you GPS a cell if you have its number?" Aaron cut back in.

"Possibly. What's happening?" Matthew actually sounded a little rattled.

"Bouchard has one of my friends. He told me to go and get Daniel's men to leave the warehouse on Miners, or he would hurt her." I could hear the near panic in my own voice.

"Hang on."

We could hear him talking, presumably on another phone. He came back to us.

"Daniel says he has only one man watching Miners. There is no one there. They are about to go find the trailer."

Aaron was trying to get my attention by tapping on my arm. Mouthing her words only, she told me she wanted my phone. As Aaron told Demi's cell number to Matthew, my racing mind suddenly came into focus.

"Bouchard is just trying to get me out of the way," I said. "The trailer may be a deception as well."

"Hold on," Matthew said, and we heard him talking on the other phone.

"Daniel's guy at Bouchard's office said a different trailer just pulled up there. Hang on." He went back to the other phone. "Two other vehicles just got there."

"That's where Daniel's guys have to go," I said. "That's where Gabriel's sister is."

"Matthew? Anything on the cell?" Aaron interrupted.

"It's off Lorne Road. Just outside the city limits."

I put the truck in gear, and the tires squealed as we shot across the boulevard and headed East.

"Tell Daniel to head to Bouchard's office. But, Matthew?"

"Yes, Max?"

"Tell them they can't hit the office until I get to Bouchard. We have to time this right. It's the only way to make sure our people don't get hurt."

"I will tell him, Max."

The eight kilometre trip around Circle Drive to Lorne Avenue felt like it took several hours, during which my heart pounded in my chest so loud I'm sure Aaron could hear it from the seat next to me. It was likely only five minutes later when I took the Lorne Avenue exit and asked Matthew, who had remained connected to us by phone, how much farther it was to Demi's cell phone. His earlier estimation, that Bouchard was just outside the city limits, turned out to be wishful thinking. In reality, he was at an acreage about fifteen kilometres out of town.

I had a powerful urge to see if I could push Aaron, myself, and the truck out of sync with time and speed the trip up some but decided that this was not the time to experiment. If something went wrong, and I wasn't able to get to Bouchard in time, I had no idea what he might do to Demi. And although it would mean we'd get there quicker, it would not make our trip feel like it went quicker, and that's what I really wanted.

"She's a pretty gutsy girl!" Aaron said, distracting me from some pretty disturbing thoughts.

"Huh?" I said.

"Smart, too," Aaron continued. "She kept her phone with her, somehow. I can't believe that Bouchard wouldn't have searched her for a phone, or had one of his guys do it, but she managed to keep it on her and keep the GPS functional."

"Fuck!" I exclaimed. "What if Bouchard had one of his guys take her phone out here? What if she's nowhere near her phone?" I'm sure I sounded every bit as panicked as I once again felt.

"Shit!" Aaron responded. "We can't think that. We have to hope she managed to keep her phone with her."

"You're getting very close, now," Matthew's voice came from the speakers. "Take the next road to the right."

We turned and drove about three kilometres west, kicking up a huge cloud of dust from the dry gravel road.

"There's an acreage off to the left just up ahead," I said to the disembodied voice.

"Judging from the GPS, that should be it," Matthew said.

"I see two cars," Aaron said. There were two large SUVs parked by a huge, beautiful stable.

"Aaron will stay in the truck and in contact with you," I said as I slammed on the brakes and pulled off the highway.

"Daniel and his men are at the Office. They're ready to…"

"Send them in," I said, and jumped out of the truck. "Stay here," I told Aaron, and pushed at time.

The acreage consisted of a large, stately house, a few smaller buildings that were nicely finished to match the house, and the large stable set back a little farther from the highway. The overall effect was one of opulence and obsessive orderliness. Not a single thing was out of place, and everything looked to be trimmed and polished. The only exception to this was a large pile of rocks behind the stable. They looked like the kind of stones one would use to build a fireplace or a rock wall and, where everything else was neatly placed, these rocks appeared to have been recently dumped there.

As I ran toward the large outbuilding, I noticed two men standing just inside its large open doors. Getting closer, I could see that doors at the other end of the building were also open, and two men stood there as well. They were far enough inside to be shaded from the sunlight hitting that side of the building, making them a little harder to spot. All four men were armed. Curled up on the wooden floor in the middle of the stable was a bound figure. Standing over her, a gun in one hand and a phone up to his ear, was Bouchard.

Slowing my run only slightly, I bent to pick up a short, piece of two-by-four from a pile of wood stacked neatly to one side of the entryway. There was a tug as I grabbed it that I felt mostly in my shoulder before the piece of wood slipped out of normal time and joined me in my out-of-sync time frame.

A moment of my time later, the two men at the front of the building were incapacitated, possibly almost decapitated, buy a single blow each from my clumsy weapon. I did not care in the least if my actions were going to leave them hospitalized, permanently injured or dead. They could have made better job choices.

As I ran past Bouchard and Demi, I saw that she was tied at

the wrists and ankles and gagged with a bright red cloth of some sort. Bouchard's mouth was open as if he was yelling something, and I got the sense that he was aware that something was happening. No doubt, he had heard the truck screeching to a stop in the yard. I considered smacking him with the board on the way by but decided against it. It seemed a better idea to deal with his men first. The two men at the back doors were dispatched before the men at the front had hit the ground. An instant later I had smacked Bouchard's gun hand and was relaxing back into normal time.

"Bouchard…" I began and, pushing back at time, stepped toward Bouchard, just as I heard the beginnings of a gunshot.

It was strange, to say the least, to hear only the start of a gunshot and to have the sound cut off as I phased out of time. It was stranger still to feel something grab my left shoulder and slowly push at it from behind. I can't imagine that being shot feels good under normal circumstances, but I have to say, it is extremely unpleasant to feel a bullet slowly push its way into your body.

The decision to disable the men at the door had been a good one, it turned out, as it left me with only one more thug to deal with other than Bouchard himself. I have him to thank for warning me that another man was there, standing in the shadows, prepared to shoot as soon as he spotted me. One would have expected a man who had just been smacked in the hand with a blow that probably broke several bones to have reacted by looking toward that hand, or the man who had caused the damage and was suddenly visible in front of him. While Bouchard had begun to look at me, he quickly shifted his focus slightly to my right, toward the sniper, before again looking back at me. It happened in a split second of regular time, but somehow, I recognized his momentary glance for what it meant. Another danger lurking in the shadows.

The impact of the bullet, or possibly the intense pain it caused, forced me back into regular time as I felt my body spin past a wide-eyed Bouchard. I hit the ground backside first and was rolled backward onto my knees by the force of the bullet. I pushed again with my mind and spotted the sniper in the corner, his elbows resting on the gate of a stall which, provided stability for the rifle in his hands. Despite the pain in my left shoulder, I took aim and threw the two-by-four board at the shooter, focusing on accuracy and letting the shift in time take care of the velocity.

Jumping to my feet, I grabbed Bouchard by one shoulder and spun him roughly toward me. I did not return to regular time. I had done so before, after disarming Bouchard, because I wanted him to be aware of the pain I was about to cause him. That choice had gotten me shot. I wouldn't make a mistake like that again. Over Bouchard's shoulder, I saw the wooden projectile make contact with the sniper in the shadows. He would definitely be needing medical attention.

I began shaking the husky man in my hands, causing his head to snap forward and back. The bound and gagged girl at our feet was lying in a fetal position facing toward us, and her eyes had grown wide as she watched the blurred activity before her. Suddenly, the man I was man-handling grabbed my shirt with both hands and began to man-handle me back. I had held on to him long enough to pull him out of time with me.

"You are a truly spectacular individual, Mr. Campbell!"

God, I hate how he says Mr. Campbell! I screamed in my mind.

"How can this be possible?" the monster said, as he continued to shake me back and forth, causing the pain in my shoulder to intensify. He must have noticed me favouring my left shoulder, as he suddenly yanked with his right hand, causing me to stumble in that direction and spinning us both around. Despite being several years older than myself, or rather older than I appeared to be, he was remarkably sturdy and strong. Of course, it was possible that I was being weakened by the pain in my shoulder, or, perhaps from a loss of blood. With some difficulty, I regained my footing and tried again to shake Bouchard.

"You fucking bastard!" I screamed at him. "If you've hurt

her I'll fucking kill you!" Yes, I was starting to lose my mind!

Suddenly Bouchard's eyes went wide, likely having noticed the sniper, who was still in the process of slowly falling to the dirt floor.

"What *is* this?" he said like we were having a casual conversation.

The guy was astoundingly unflappable. Summoning more will, I pushed against him with all my strength in a renewed attempt to flap him. I managed to shake him back and forth again, but his large body seemed to absorb my efforts without ill effect.

"How is it you are doing this, Mr. Campbell?"

I bellowed like an animal, and shaking him again, I tried to spin him at the same time. We spun halfway around, and Bouchard finally lost his footing and fell toward me. Remembering a professional wrestling move I'd seen many times on TV, I pulled down on Bouchard as I fell backward, at the same time catching his weight on my right foot and levering him over me, intending him to land painfully on his back in the hard dirt. As an incredible pain shot through my shoulder, Bouchard flipped over me, and I released him. Only then did I remember what happened to the rock I had thrown by the river a few days earlier.

Relaxing time, I sat up and reached out toward Demi, intending to remove her gag to see if she was okay. As I did so, I glanced up and saw that the two-by-four board I had bounced off the sniper was still floating slowly through the air.

What the hell?

Looking back at Demi, I again made the conscious relaxing effort to return to regular time. The girl was still not moving. I tried again.

Suddenly, many things happened at once. The board I used to take out the gunman bounced off the inside wall of the building as the gunman himself hit the floor. A microsecond later, there was a deafening BOOM, as dust was shaken from every part of the building and dirt from the floor flew into the air as the ground itself shook. Combined with all of this was a crashing sound like that of an exploding brick wall that came from the large rear doors of the stable, the direction in which I had tossed Bouchard. Believing the building itself might be falling down, I threw myself over Demi, where I stayed until the dust settled.

"'Gemmoffmmee!'" a muffled voice beneath me ordered. My internal universal translator rendered it as, "Get off me!"

I lifted myself off of Demi, my shoulder burning with every movement. She levered her body, managing to get into a sitting position in front of me. I reached out with my right hand and removed the gag from her mouth.

"Jesus, Max! I thought you were going to crush me to death."

'You're welcome!' I thought. "Sorry," I said, starting to work on her ankle bindings. It occurred to me that she may not be aware that I just saved her. It all had happened rather quickly.

"Max! Have you been shot?"

"Uh, yeah, I guess," I replied. Grunting and sweating, I managed to remove the ropes from her wrists. "My truck is out front. A friend of mine is in it. Wait for me there. Please," I added.

Rubbing her wrists, Demi began to limp toward the large opening at the front of the stable. At the entryway, she bent and removed something from the jacket pocket of one of the two guards.

Looking back at me, she held up what she had retrieved, but silhouetted in the doorway as she was, I couldn't make it out.

I turned toward the large opening at the rear. As I passed the two fallen goons, I stooped and checked each for a pulse. As best I could tell, they were both alive. Beyond that, I couldn't bring myself to care. I continued on through the door and out to the large rock pile beyond.

What I found was not so much a rock pile as a rock field. What had been a roughly seven-foot-high pile of rocks was now much smaller. Beyond it was a large area of scattered and mostly shattered stones. Slight discolouration on the surface of some of the rocks was all that appeared to be left of the human projectile that had smashed them.

Feeling slightly sickened, I turned and walked around the large metal building and headed to the truck. I did not bother to check on the health of the other three men.

Aaron and Demi ran to me when they saw me approaching. Aaron did what she could to help me, lifting my right arm and putting it over her tiny shoulders. Demi, who was on my left, made several motions as if to help, but seemingly couldn't decide how to do so without touching my injured shoulder. She finally ran ahead and opened a rear door on the truck. They helped me into the back seat, and I fell over to lay on my uninjured side. Demi had jumped into the driver's seat.

"Matthew, Max has been shot!" Aaron shouted as she hopped into the front passenger seat.

It was the last thing I heard before I passed out.

CHAPTER TWENTY-FOUR

I woke in a dimly lit room. Looking around trying to place my surroundings, I was pleasantly surprised to find Demi resting next to me. She lay on her back to my right with her beautiful face turned toward me.

'I think I'm in heaven, Elsie!'

'Not yet, Orville. They still need you down there.'

Glancing down, I noticed that Demi was wearing a simple white T-shirt like the one I'd been reborn in not many weeks before. I couldn't recall a T-shirt ever looking so fabulous.

"Eyes up here, Buddy."

Damn! Caught!

"Are you sure you haven't already developed anti-gravity," I said without looking up.

Demi giggled and poked me in the side, which reminded me that I'd been shot. It was like being stabbed in the shoulder with a hot poker. I winced but managed to keep from crying.

"Sorry," Demi whispered.

"Where are we?"

"Rebellion House."

"What time is it?"

She picked up her cell phone, which had been resting happily on her tummy, and blinded us both by turning on its screen.

"Almost three AM," she responded, once her eyes had adjusted. "Go back to sleep."

She rolled toward me and snuggled in, her hand resting lightly on my chest. She kissed me gently on the cheek.

What hot poker? I thought, and with a smile on my face I drifted off to sleep.

When I woke again, Demi was gone. A breeze from a partially opened window had freshened the air in the room, and I could hear birds singing outside. I lay still for a few minutes and watched the curtains moving in the breeze. They would slowly expand into the room, then separate and fall back to the window where they would close and then start to extend inward again. It was very peaceful and, oddly, rather like watching the universe breathe. The natural rhythm of it gave me the sense that everything was right with the world.

I felt my left shoulder with my right hand and found tape there holding a bandage in place. I managed to swing my legs off the bed and sit up despite the searing pain it caused in my shoulder. *How can a little hole hurt so much?* On a chair close by lay a pair of jeans and a black T-shirt. My boots were on the floor next to the chair with a new pair of socks draped over them.

I stood up, but stayed next to the bed, waiting for a slight dizziness to pass, and then proceeded to wrestle the jeans on, managing the entire process one-handed. The socks were a bit more of a challenge, and I had to use my teeth to remove a sticky band that held them together at the top. At one point I had it stuck and hanging from my chin and was glad that there was no one there to see it. I got the socks in place and stuffed my feet into my boots, not bothering to do them up.

The T-shirt was going to be another matter. I managed to slide it up my left arm without too much discomfort and then, gritting my teeth, pulled the thing over my head and forced my right arm into the other sleeve. The process wasn't much more painful than I expected. Comparable to cutting your fingers off. With scissors. One at a time. But I didn't cry. I'm pretty grown up for a ninety-one-year-old. I picked up my cell phone from the nightstand next to the bed.

There was a full-length mirror in the corner by the door, and I checked myself out. I didn't look bad considering the black T-shirt highlighted the sickly pallidness of my complexion. I noted with a certain pride that the shirt bore the unique Rebellion logo.

Bet that's a first! I thought, and went in search of intelligent life.

At the end of a corridor, I found a narrow set of stairs and, descending, I found myself in a kitchen where a large woman was elbows deep in a sink, washing pots. She was humming happily.

"Hi," I said, causing her to jump and splash water up onto the counter.

"Max, you're up!" she said, giving me a huge smile. "How are you feeling?"

"Uh, good, good," I replied. "Uh, who…"

"Mary," she replied. "I'm Matthew and Daniel's mother."

"Hey! Nice to meet you!" I'd be lying if I said I wasn't surprised to find the Bird Brother's mother happily toiling in Rebellion's kitchen. "My girl, uh, Demi was here earlier…"

"She had a class to attend. She left a couple of hours ago. Asked me to have you text her when you got up and said she'd call when she can. Are you hungry? I can make you something."

I was famished but didn't want to put her to any trouble.

"Uh, yeah. Cereal would be great!"

Mary set a cup of coffee in front of me, and I lowered myself slowly into a chair. As she went about placing several boxes of cereal on the table, along with a jug of milk and a bowl, I took a moment to text Demi.

'Thanks for being there for me.'

"Is Daniel here, Mary?" I asked.

"He went downtown to see Matthew. You should give him a call when you're done breakfast."

I picked out a box of Quaker Harvest Crunch from more than a dozen options provided by my hostess and emptied half of it into my bowl. Filling the remaining space with milk, I proceeded to shovel it into my face. It was one of the best meals I ever had. My cell buzzed as I was ladling the last of the milk into my mouth. I could read Demi's response without picking the phone up from the table.

'DITTO! TTYL' I told myself to ask Aaron about that last one, but then the translation popped into my head.

"Who bandaged me up, Mary?"

"Daniel's friend. She's a doctor at St.Paul's. She came here when they brought you in."

"So, do you know what happened with Daniel and his guys yesterday? HEY! Classes? Is it Monday?" My brain cells were responding to the intake of calories.

"Yes. Sheri, that's Daniel's friend, pumped you full of drugs to help you sleep," Mary poured more coffee in my cup and took my bowl away. "And, yes, I heard what happened, but Daniel would be upset if I don't let him tell you."

At that moment Aaron came in, shrieked and threw herself

at me, wrapping her little arms around me and squeezing with surprising strength. I gritted my teeth and accepted it without complaint. I'm a pretty tough guy.

"I think we could have stood back and let Gabriel take care of all of them," Daniel said.

We were sitting at a large table in Clark's Crossing Brew Pub, in an area that not many years ago was the westernmost edge of the city. Daniel was there with Sheri, the Doctor who took care of my injured shoulder and who was a pretty, long-haired brunette. Next to Matthew sat a lean woman with short dark hair named Lori. She was, I was surprised to learn, his wife. She and Aaron, who was in her young lady persona, ignored most of the conversation and spent their time looking at Lori's baby pictures. Also at the table was Earl, the huge acne-scarred man I'd first encountered outside WonderWall nightclub, and his girlfriend Charlene, a big-boned girl who was at least as tall as her date. The way they kept looking at each other, I was pretty sure they were about to start the production of their own little army of black-haired giants. Sitting next to them, and looking even smaller than usual because of it, was Detective Corporal Corey Tkatchuk. At my right sat the prettiest girl I'd known in two lifetimes.

"As it was, it took two of our own guys to keep Gabriel from killing anybody," Earl said.

"Good thing, too! When I got there, the other cops were getting ready to put you guys in handcuffs." Corey told him. "If any of Bouchard's men were seriously injured, I don't think any of you would have gone home that night."

"Nonetheless, we are grateful to you, Corey," Daniel said. "Without your help, Gabriel might well have been arrested for abducting his own sister. Without you, we would have been hard-pressed to get the cops to even listen to our side of the story."

"I'm sorry that's still the way it is," the young detective said.

"Well, despite what you might think, many of us are working to change that," said Matthew.

"Well, all I can say is, it's a good thing Daniel had the forethought to call me before you guys started bashing heads."

"I never heard what happened to you," Earl said, addressing me.

The table went quiet for a moment as everyone waited to see how I'd respond. Obviously, Earl hadn't got the message that we'd be avoiding my part of the story for the duration of our group-meeting-slash-dinner-party.

"Nothing Earl," I responded. "We found the tracker I was following laying in the ditch."

Earl and Corey both seemed to be satisfied with my answer and neither noticed Daniel smile at me briefly then glance away.

"Can I see those pictures too?" Demi asked Lori and Aaron.

With that, the seating arrangement was reshuffled so that all five women could make goo-goo eyes at a cell phone. The men continued our 'debriefing' of the raid on Bouchard's office. I learned that they'd hit the men there so quietly and quickly that the few shots that Bouchard's guys managed to get off went wild and hit no one. They subdued six men, including the semi-driver and were holding them in the front office when four police cars arrived. Even though the boys of Rebellion exhibited empty hands to the excited officers and pointed to a wastebasket full of guns they'd confiscated from Bouchard's thugs, the police were preparing to arrest Daniel's men and let the others go when Detective Tkatchuk showed up. Corey was only able to convince the other cops who the true bad guys were when Daniel suggested they check out the trailer's false front. Fortunately, a check of the registration proved the semi was owned by one of Bouchard's companies.

From behind the trailer's false wall, the police freed four young women who were all gagged, bound, and drugged.

Gabriel's sister was one of them. When she was untied, and immediately threw her arms around her brother and began sobbing, the police turned their entire attention to Bouchard's guys.

"Do you think the circumstances, catching Bouchard's men red-handed at his office, will give you enough to press charges against him?" I asked Corey.

"We'll be reviewing the case over the next few days, but I wouldn't get your hopes up to high. Every one of Bouchard's guys is wanted for one thing or another, so we'll put them away for something, but I don't know about their boss. I think the pressure from the department to lay off Bouchard will stop, but until we can find him and question him, I really can't guess how things are going to go."

"We need to focus on finding out who was buying the girls from Bouchard," I said to Cory. "We could start by finding out where the driver was taking the girls."

"Gee, Sherlock! Good idea!" the detective chided. "We've already talked to the driver, and he gave us a location and some names of people in BC. Smith has his people out there looking into it."

The conversation shifted to other subjects, breaking into smaller groups as conversations in larger groups tend to do. At one point I heard Earl, Lori and Daniel discussing gay relationships with the young detective. From what I could gather, Corey had recently begun dating a new man, and the others ribbed him for not bringing him along. Demi, Aaron, Matthew and Sheri had a lengthy discussion about the future of artificial intelligence. After a couple of unsuccessful attempts to join that conversation, I joined one on young kids and cell phone addiction that had branched off from it.

Daniel and Matthew poured coke into themselves like caffeine was their primary fuel source, I'd seen nothing to make me think otherwise, and the rest of us, girls included, made a respectable dent in the bar's draft beer supply. The food, when it came, was good, but it could have been cardboard for all anyone paid attention to it. With all of the talking and laughing going on, the food vanished without anyone taking time out to comment on either its arrival or subsequent disappearance. Two and a half hours later, with the intended purpose of expressing the group's gratitude to Detective Tkatchuk accomplished, Matthew insisted on paying the bill, and we headed home.

Demi's next couple of days were filled with classes, so I dropped her off before heading home with Aaron. In the hallway outside her apartment, she made me promise we would 'talk' when I took her for dinner two evenings hence. She then gave me a kiss goodnight which convinced me that she, too, had a unique ability to alter the flow of time.

"I can't stand it anymore!" Aaron shouted, as soon as I was back in the truck. "What happened? What did you do to Bouchard? What was that explosion? Did they have a bazooka or something?" She might have kept going indefinitely, so I spoke the two words I thought had the best chance of slowing her down.

"Bouchard's dead."

"Holy fuck!" Aaron said slowly, emphasizing each syllable equally.

"I don't think there's enough of him left to be identified."

I spent the trip back to our place telling her what happened after I left her in the truck. Once in the apartment we each grabbed a beer and took our favourite spots in the living room.

"I haven't had an opportunity to test my theory yet, but I guess I can slow time down more than I realized," I said. "When I was hurt and wrestling with Bouchard, and we were pushing each other back and forth, I think I was pushing at time over and over again without realizing I was doing it."

"Huh?" Aaron wasn't following me.

"I was in shock from the bullet wound, I guess, and it was taking a lot of mental effort to keep fighting that bastard. He was stronger than you might imagine, and I was getting weaker.

Also, he kept talking like he was in a frigging board-meeting. He had to be completely insane, that guy!

"Anyway," I said it slowly and carefully because I didn't want Aaron's autocorrect to kick in, "It took considerable effort to keep fighting him. He had slipped 'Out of Time' with me because we were in prolonged contact, and it seems that every time I forced myself mentally to renew my physical efforts against him, I gave the same mental 'push' that moves me out of sync with regular time. Each time I did that it caused both of us to move farther out of time. When I used the wrestling maneuver to throw him off of me and then let go of him, he re-entered regular time. But because he was moving, when he re-entered he was actually moving at many times the speed of sound, I would guess. That was the explosion you heard or at least part of it. A sonic boom. The other part was his body hitting the rock pile. The two things would have happened so fast that it would have sounded like the same explosion. I don't know for sure, because I didn't hear it. I hadn't totally returned to regular time. I thought I did because I'd made the mental relaxing effort that usually brings me back, but then I noticed that everything was still slowed down around me. So, I 'relaxed' again. It was only after I did it three or four times that I re-entered regular time. The only other possibility is that I'm losing the ability to come back into the normal time flow and that's a terrifying thought."

Aaron didn't say anything, but her face displayed a slightly terror-stricken expression.

"But I don't think that's the case," I continued in the hope of reassuring her. It had the added benefit of reassuring me as well. "Bouchard's body was completely obliterated. And the rock pile wasn't just scattered. Most of the rocks were shattered as well. For that to have happened, he would have had to have been moving much faster than I was when I tried to run on top of the water."

"So, his body is never going to be found, then?"

"I don't think there's anything left of his body to be found.

Even his clothing seems to have been destroyed."

"What about the guards he had with him? What about them?"

"I don't think I killed any of them, but I'm not totally sure about that. I've been checking the news, but other than people hearing a loud bang that no one can explain, there hasn't been anything else mentioned."

"Social media went crazy about the bang for a couple of days," Aaron said, "but nobody was able to figure out where it came from. People lose interest pretty fast."

"If I ever get involved with this kind of thing again, I'm going to have to find a better way of dealing with bad guys than bashing their heads in. I can't bring myself to feel bad about Bouchard, he was a psychotic son-of-a-bitch. But I'm not a killer. At least, I don't want to be."

"Do you think it's all over, then?" Aaron asked.

"Probably not completely," I said after a pause. "The people Bouchard was selling the girls to are still out there, so they have to be found and stopped. And I think it's been going on for a lot longer than people realize. But I'm not sure that I need to get involved in cleaning up the whole mess, we have cops for that. I need to take some time to figure out what's going on. I still don't know why I'm here or why I have these crazy powers."

"With great power comes great responsibility," Aaron said, quoting a famous line from the Spiderman comic books.

"I ran a printing press for forty years. I don't think that prepared me for 'Great Responsibility'. The funny thing is, the thing I can't get out of my mind the last couple of days is, what's going to happen to my Penthouse? With Bouchard missing, what's going to happen to the Meewasin Landing Project?"

Aaron got up and got us two more beer. I was already feeling the effects of the alcohol and probably shouldn't have even driven home. All the beer this little girl was drinking must have been going to the same place the enormous amounts of food she eats went. It didn't seem to be having any effect on her.

"What about Corey and the RCMP guy? Won't it seem strange to them if you suddenly lose interest in the missing girls?"

"I talked with Corey and told him to keep me posted and let me know if there is anything he thinks I can do. He may want me to go back out east, or maybe Vancouver, to do more poking around. If so, I may have to bring you along to keep you out of trouble."

"If you don't bring me, I promise, there will be trouble," the tiny girl said, dryly. "What about Demi? Didn't she see you fighting with Bouchard?"

"I don't think she knows what she saw. I haven't decided yet just what I'm going to tell her."

Aaron laughed. "Buddy-boy, I think you'll tell her everything she wants to know.

CHAPTER TWENTY-FIVE

"How old do you think I am?"

"Well, you look younger to me, but based on your education you must be at least twenty-five." Demi had no idea how hard it was for me to judge ages in anyone under fifty.

"Good try! You missed it by that much," She held her hand up with thumb and forefinger almost touching. "But my education isn't a good way to judge. I finished high school two years early, but Mom and Dad wouldn't let me go right into University. I stayed home for a year and took some correspondence classes. And, I've been squeezing in more than a normal workload each year."

"So?" I prompted.

"Twenty-four," she said with a big, beautiful smile lighting up her face. "But I've been told I look older, which doesn't really thrill me very much. So, how old are you?"

She looked up at me with those bright blue eyes, and I came to a decision.

"I'll be ninety-two next month."

I know it was nearly the same line I'd used when I told Aaron, but it was a great line, and I'd never get to it often enough for it to grow old. Demi stared at me with absolutely no expression on her face until I became uncomfortable with the silence.

"Well?" I prodded.

"Seriously. How old?"

"I'm ninety-one years old."

"You are totally serious, aren't you?"

We had enjoyed a fantastic meal at The Keg on 8th Street, and the entire time I was amazed at the poise and beauty of this young woman. Everyone in the restaurant stole glances at her at some point during our meal. Some people openly stared. When she got up to 'powder her nose' the restaurant went noticeably quiet as the patrons watched her go by. Despite the effect her appearance had on everyone, she seemed oblivious. She smiled and chatted with the wait staff, taking pains to make a waitress-in-training feel comfortable and appreciated. It was more than just one waitress recognizing the nervousness of 'the new girl'. She genuinely liked people, and everyone she met could feel it. As a result, everyone she met was a bit happier to have come in contact with her. We had talked and laughed through the entire meal, and I couldn't remember ever feeling prouder to be with someone.

'Sorry, Elsie!'

'It's okay, Orville. I like her too!'

During the evening, the conversation had hiccuped a couple of times, the result of my not being up to date on life as it pertains to twenty-something people in this day and age. Once I made reference to a long-cancelled TV show and then stammered something about watching reruns. Another time I very nearly made reference to one of my grandchildren and stopped talking mid-sentence while my brain went in search of some way to make it sound natural. I never managed to come up with anything, and so just sat there looking like I'd suffered a brain hemorrhage. Each time the conversation stuttered, Demi picked up the flow and brushed past it like it hadn't happened. She was poised, intelligent, quick-witted and, in case I forgot to mention it, an absolute wonder to look at. It was her open kindness with strangers and her willingness to accept everything about me, including my obvious, unexplainable oddities, plus the fact that I liked her too much to be anything but upfront with her, that helped me decide to tell her the truth.

"I know it's crazy, but it's the truth. My real name is Orville Olsen, and I'm ninety-one years old."

At hearing my name, her eyes lit up, and an expression of wonder filled her face, no doubt remembering the name from the first day we met. When I had returned to the bar a few days later I had asked her to 'Just call me Max', and she accepted the new name without question.

"It does make a strange sort of sense. I mean, I did wonder. But how? Don't you age like everyone else?"

The next couple of hours passed with Demi asking questions and me answering the ones I could. It was soon apparent that, of all the people in my current world, she was the one who most deserved to know my secrets. With her education and brilliant mind, she was also the one who stood the best chance of helping me find answers. Her excitement and wonder were a pure pleasure for me, but her demeanour cooled when she learned the fate of Bouchard.

"I didn't mean to kill him. I wasn't totally aware of what was happening at the time," I said, desperately afraid of losing her approval.

"I'm not judging you, Max! Henry Bouchard was an evil man, and the world is better off without him. I'm more worried about how killing him might affect you. You might not be exactly the man I thought you were, but one thing I know for sure is that you are a good man. And a nice man. You may still be in shock. There may be stuff you still need to deal with."

"I'm okay, I think," I replied, very much relieved. "Hey! What did you take from that guy's pocket in the stable? The guard. As you were leaving."

"Oh! My cell phone. When they grabbed me, I knew they would probably search me, and if they found it, they'd take it away or maybe leave it behind. I knew it was one way someone might be able to track us, so I put it in his pocket as they were carrying me down the stairs."

"You are absolutely amazing!" I told her. This girl is so wonderful she makes my heart hurt. "But, Demi, you totally accepted my whole story like you've heard it all before. You didn't even question my claim that I alter time."

Demi thought for a moment before answering, taking time to put her thoughts in order.

"Max, I believe you think you are ninety-one years old. I believe you think you died and were reborn in a new body. And I think you believe that you can see people's future. But I suspect there may be some other answer. There might be something that explains how you came to believe this. But when it comes to your ability to alter the flow of time, I'm pretty sure that other things are going on. I hate to say it, but you might have a brain tumour or possibly something more serious. We should take you to see a doctor."

I was smiling at her as she said this. Of course, she would question everything I'd told her. She was a scientist. Quite possibly the smartest student ever to attend the University of Saskatchewan. It was totally understandable that she would look for answers that fit the things she knew about the physical universe. I was smiling because I knew I could get her to see the universe in a new way.

I slowly took my arm from around her shoulders, we had

been sitting in her loveseat, and she was snuggled up against me, and as soon as we were no longer in contact, I pushed at time. For good measure, and because I hadn't had a chance to test my new theory, I pushed at it a second time. The world went completely silent, as I had come to expect, and I got up from my seat and stepped away. The cushion where I'd been seated was still crushed as if an invisible ninety-kilogram man was sitting in it. Demi appeared to be completely frozen. I walked to the hallway leading to her bedroom and, peeking around the corner to see her reaction, I let time relax back to normal.

"Holy Crap!" Demi screamed with a mixture of shock and excitement.

"Hi there," I said, from the hallway.

Demi very nearly jumped through the balcony window behind her. Pushing time again, but this time only once, I walked over and got down on one knee in front of her and then relaxed time again.

"Will you be my girlfriend, Demi?" I asked.

"Jesus Christ! You scared the...what? Yes. Yes, I'll be your girlfriend," She said as she threw herself at me, knocking me onto my back and landing on top of me. She started a kiss designed to break down all of my defenses and then stopped and pulled her face away from mine. "Are you sure you want to date someone seventy years younger than you? Doesn't that make you a dirty old man or something."

"At the moment, I can't think of a better reason for coming back to life," I said.

Over the next few hours, we made our way from her living room floor into her bedroom. I found myself considering something that Aaron had asked me a few days earlier. We were having one of our many meals together when she asked me which of my new powers I thought was the best one. At the time I had answered it was the ability to shift time. I told her that seeing people futures was not only uncomfortable at the best of times, but it was also the one that led to all kinds of problems. Shifting time, however, tended to be the power that helps me to solve problems.

However, up to the point when Aaron asked that question, the flashes I'd received had always been of emotionally powerful events that people were about to experience at some point in their near future. The time I shook hands with Brad-The-Salesman, his flash took me only several minutes ahead to the moment I agreed to purchase the Penthouse. Never before had the most significant emotional event a flash participant was soon to experience been one taking place at the exact instant we came in contact.

When I found myself in the arms of this remarkable young woman, I experienced something I didn't realize could happen. It seems that the most emotionally exceptional experience Demi would have was actually happening at that very place and time, and possibly because it was happening there and then, I was experiencing the event as if I occupied both bodies. Sharing it with her was like having an emotional and physical feedback system explicitly designed to enhance our experience together. Not only did I have the pleasure of having her amazing body in my arms, but at the same instant, I could feel precisely how much she was enjoying being there. I knew exactly how every movement I made affected her, and her enjoyment served to increase every aspect of my own. But even more amazing to me was the sense that I wasn't losing contact with my own body during this flash. In the past, while experiencing someone's future, I felt and saw only what my flash partner would be seeing and feeling. It always seemed that, during a flash, my own body didn't exist. But this ongoing flash with Demi was different. It was as if I was sharing her experience while simultaneously experiencing it through my own senses. However, that was not the most remarkable effect of the experience.

As with every flash, the reception of my flash partner's emotions is always the most powerful element. It is, I believe, the very thing that triggers a flash in the first place and it is often the thing that remains with me after the vision is over. Frequently it is embarrassing for me, as in those flashes where I share another's intimate exploits. Sometimes it is exciting, like sharing the enjoyment of a big game win or reading the numbers on a winning lottery ticket. And sometimes it's upsetting, as in learning of a death in the family or, as in the case of Henry Bouchard, feeling his despicable enjoyment of an activity that a healthy mind would find revolting. But in this unprecedented experience, the emotions that I received were powerfully uplifting. Like myself, Demi was undergoing the most amazing, powerful, life-changing experience and nothing can adequately describe how it felt, except perhaps to say that it filled us both to overflowing and still continued to grow. In almost one hundred years, after a wonderful marriage to a remarkable woman, after two children, five grandchildren and nine great-grandchildren, and after uncountable friends had come and gone, I can safely say that I had never experienced an emotion as all-encompassing as the love I felt at that moment. And perhaps most remarkable of all, I knew from what I felt from her, that she was receiving the same emotions reflected back to her from me, as clearly and as powerfully as if she also had this unbelievable power of perception. Needless to say, it completely changed my mind about which of my unusual abilities was the better one.

Not for the first time that evening, Demi wrapped her arms around me and squeezed me to her. Our bodies shuddered in unison. I was so overcome with pure joy I felt I might die. For real, this time.

Yep. Best power, ever! I thought.

EPILOGUE

"What the hell? Who're You? How'd you get in here?" the startled man asked.

Of course, I'd come in through the door with him, squeezing past with time slowed down a couple of notches. Before rejoining the normal flow of time, I'd found a big comfy chair to sit in, so he would find me there, in the dark room, waiting for him. It was a total cliché. It was exactly what I was going for. It was nice of him to give me some equally clichéd responses.

"I'll ask the questions here," I said. I know. No originality there either. "Are you John Bantle?"

"Yeah. Who the fuck are you?"

"Okay, well, I guess I don't have any more questions, so we'll go with yours. I'm a friend of your girlfriend's daughter."

I guess John couldn't tell, with him standing and me sitting, that I was bigger and in much better shape than him, because he suddenly threw himself at me. I'm not sure what he planned to accomplish with that maneuver but, since I wasn't in the chair when he got there, he accomplished going ass-over-teakettle onto the floor with the chair landing on top of him. When he looked up, he found me sitting on the sofa across the room.

"Like I was saying, I'm a friend of Aaron's, but you can call me the 'Ghost of Christmas Future'."

John had gotten out from under the chair, and as he attempted to get to his feet, he reached out for a small table for support. My 'Inner Child' slowed time and moved the table out of his grasp. The result was perfect. He was once again sprawled on the floor.

"If you could just refrain from falling all over the place for a minute, I'll explain why I'm here."

Bantle grunted as he got onto his hands and knees.

"I'm here to tell you that I know what a sick son of a bitch you are and that, unless you want to spend all of your future Christmases in a wheelchair, you'll never go anywhere near that girl again."

"I've never touched that girl," he said. He'd managed to get to his feet.

Slowing time only a little, so he would see my movements as a blur, I moved from where I was sitting to standing right in front of him and, resuming regular time, I slapped him as hard as I could. It turned out that was pretty hard, and it spun him half around and sent him face first into the corner where, again, he had to pick himself up off the floor. When he did so, he found me on the sofa once again, flipping through a hunting magazine.

"What the fuck?" His voice was filled with a combination of frustration and fear. He made a sudden lunge to another corner of the room and tripped over a heavy coffee table that suddenly appeared in front of him. When he looked up from the floor, I was holding the baseball bat he'd been going for.

"Jesus Christ!" He sounded scared.

"In fact, if I ever hear of you causing any woman grief, I might just come back and rip your legs right off and mail bits of them back to you every Christmas for the rest of your life." I know that was a little much, but I wanted to keep the Christmas theme going. "Or maybe I should just let your fellow officers know what an absolute bastard you are."

There he was, a grown man and an RCMP officer, and he looked like he was about to burst into tears. No, he looked like he might do something even more embarrassing.

When Aaron's mother came to visit for the first time, and I had learned that her boyfriend was going to take advantage of the 'alone-time' to head up to his cabin for the week, it seemed like the perfect time for him and me to have a little chat. I'd hopped in the truck early that morning to make sure I'd get there before him. He didn't keep me waiting very long, not that I would have minded the wait. The cooling air and shorter days had begun the autumn colour shift, and I could have sat there all day enjoying the scenery.

"How the fuck...? How are you doing this?" He was really spooked.

This was so much fun!

"I told you. I'm a ghost. And I promise you. If you ever touch another girl, if you ever do anything you wouldn't want your own mother to know about, anything, I'll know about it, and I'll come back and do more than just haunt you. I'll cause you so much pain you'll wish you were a ghost yourself." Okay. That was better.

I picked Bantle up off the floor and put him back on his feet, then pretended to dust off his shoulders.

"Do you understand what I'm telling you, Bantle?"

"Yeah. Yeah, I understand." He was very pale and was shaking noticeably.

I slowed time briefly, so it appeared to him I'd teleported back to the front door of the small cabin.

"Don't make me come see you again." I opened the door and began to go through it, then changing my mind, walked back over and kicked him in the nuts.

'Well, Elsie. I may just have to apologize to Aaron's mother for that last bit.'

'He deserved much worse than that, Orville. You let him off easy.'

'You always were a lot tougher than me, my dear."

As I drove away, I thought about all I'd been through since going out for that early morning drive a few short weeks ago. I thought about the new life I was building and the extraordinary people who were a part of it. I had a lot of challenges ahead. There were so many unanswered questions. How did I come to be reborn? Why was I able to see people's future? Why was I able to shift myself outside of the normal flow of time? The three answers were linked in some way, but that didn't give me the first idea of how such incredible things could happen.

There were other challenges as well. Something still had to be done about the human trafficking ring. It was certain that, with the death of Bouchard, the Saskatoon branch of that organization had received a setback, but the organization still existed and was no doubt still going strong in other parts of Canada, and possibly the United States and Mexico as well. Could I use my new gifts to shut it all down? Is that why I'm still here?

And then there was my great-granddaughter Jenny. I was still troubled by her choice of income supplementation. Why couldn't she have gotten a waitressing job like most girls her age? Doesn't she realize how dangerous her activities could be? Is it any of my business? Do I have the right to get involved? I didn't have answers for any of these questions.

I had lived a typical mundane life for over ninety years, if not always choosing the easiest path, then certainly choosing the safe one. Since my rebirth I found myself thrust into a life where there were no safe paths, and I was forced to admit that I now felt more alive than I'd ever felt before.

By the time I'd reached the highway, the autumn air had warmed enough that I could lower the truck windows and enjoy the fragrance of freshly harvested fields. I had some sixties music playing on the stereo. I pointed the truck South and headed back to Saskatoon.

It was great to be alive. Again.

The End

The story continues in
Book Two of **About Time**!

Visit

www.mark-savage.com

and join the mailing list to be notified when
About Time
Continues.

ABOUT THE AUTHOR

As the single father of quintuplets, Mark struggled not just to put food on the table, but to find a single bedtime tale with which to lull all five children to sleep. Failing in his search, he began writing the About Time series of stories. He now spends his nights dreaming that, like J.K. Rowling, his books will become international bestsellers and that he, too, might live his declining years in opulence, making fun of Donald Trump. Mark Savage is a pen name.

Made in the USA
Middletown, DE
26 July 2019